To: Mom
Enjoy!
Love, Kim

christmas
CATS
a literary companion

christmas CATS

a literary companion

EDITED AND WITH AN INTRODUCTION
BY SHIRLEY ROUSSEAU MURPHY

Chamberlain Bros.
a member of Penguin Group (USA) Inc.
New York

CHAMBERLAIN BROS.
Published by the Penguin Group
Penguin Group (USA) Inc., 375 Hudson Street, New York, New York 10014, USA •
Penguin Group (Canada), 90 Eglinton Avenue East, Suite 700, Toronto, Ontario M4P
2Y3, Canada (a division of Pearson Penguin Canada Inc.) • Penguin Books Ltd, 80
Strand, London WC2R 0RL, England • Penguin Ireland, 25 St Stephen's Green, Dublin
2, Ireland (a division of Penguin Books Ltd) • Penguin Group (Australia), 250
Camberwell Road, Camberwell, Victoria 3124, Australia (a division of Pearson Australia
Group Pty Ltd) • Penguin Books India Pvt Ltd, 11 Community Centre, Panchsheel
Park, New Delhi–110 017, India • Penguin Group (NZ), Cnr Airborne and Rosedale
Roads, Albany, Auckland 1310, New Zealand (a division of Pearson New Zealand Ltd)
• Penguin Books (South Africa) (Pty) Ltd, 24 Sturdee Avenue, Rosebank, Johannesburg
2196, South Africa • Penguin Books Ltd, Registered Offices: 80 Strand, London WC2R
0RL, England

Published simultaneously in Canada

Library of Congress Cataloging-in-Publication Data
Christmas cats : a literary companion / edited and with an introduction by Shirley
Rousseau Murphy.
      p. cm.
   ISBN 1-59609-155-X
   1. Christmas—Literary collections. 2. Cats—Literary collections.
   3. American literature. 4. English literature. I. Murphy, Shirley Rousseau.

PS509.C56C524 2005   2005045535
810.8'0334—dc22

Printed in the United States of America
10 9 8 7 6 5 4 3 2 1

A complete list of credits and permissions appears on pages 244–245.

Book design by Melissa Gerber

While the author has made every effort to provide accurate telephone numbers and
Internet addresses at the time of publication, neither the publisher nor the author
assumes any responsibility for errors, or for changes that occur after publication. Further,
the publisher does not have any control over and does not assume any responsibility for
author or third-party websites or their content.

Contents

Introduction

SHIRLEY ROUSSEAU MURPHY

From feline sleuth to denizen of organized crime to television star—all of them sharp clawed and blessed with satisfying purrs—the cats in this collection offer Christmas stories to fit your every mood. If you will heed Wendy Christensen's advice to spend at least part of your holiday curled up before a blazing fire with your cat and a good book, these tales offer laughter, wonder, and sometimes tears—but always a happy ending to add a touch of magic to your Christmas.

Memories of long ago Christmases when I was a child bring back that quiet magic for me—long rainy afternoons reading a wonderful story, snuggled with one cat or another; quiet times when I could touch other worlds and other lives, all woven in with the family rituals of the holiday season.

There were always cats at Christmas, sleeping beneath our decorated tree or beside the hearth, young kitties batting at ornaments while the older, more sedate fellows shared holiday snuggles and bits of our turkey. My first two cats were a Christmas gift when I was six: a pair of black kittens offered by my kindergarten teacher who, desperate to find takers for the big litter, recognized an easy mark in my pet-loving mother. Gracie and Charlie lived very well in our house, indulging in ample petting and warm beds. They received gift-wrapped toy mice at Christmas, and new blankets tied with bows. After their deaths there was a long succession of other beloved house cats, among them gray-and-white Skipper who, on a cold December day, brought home with him a young, thin stray; Skipper leaped and clawed at the screen door until we let the starveling in and fed him. Of course that tabby cat never left. He shared many Christmases with us, and he and Skipper remained pals. We named him Hungry, which he always was, and he grew up large and sleek and very mellow, after his rough beginning.

My father trained horses, and at our stable, several miles away, little gray Peggy appeared on another wet winter day; winter is hard on a small, homeless animal. She, too, was a starveling. She, too, soon grew fat and sleek. Peggy became our prize mouser; but it was jackrabbits that challenged her. Early mornings, she would leave her current litter of kittens in the hay barn and follow my father into the pastures when he irrigated, wading up to her belly in water as she watched for jackrabbits escaping from their flooded holes. Dispatching her quarry quickly, she would drag a rabbit as big as herself back through the water for long distances, to give to her babies. Over the years, my parents found homes for dozens of Peggy's children. In those days, no one thought of neutering a cat. I don't like to think how many unwanted kittens led a hard and homeless life or died alone—but not the cats my parents befriended. My mother and father respected our cats as they did our working dogs and horses; they understood that all animals bring to our lives a deeper dimension. I knew that gentle magic in the company of our animals, just as I did in the rituals of Christmas. Humankind's fascination with all the mysteries of life—from the inexplicable knowledge we see in the eyes of a species other than our own, to the greatest mystery of all, the mystery of Christ's birth—springs from the same deep genetic hunger to touch the unknown.

Mankind's every invention owes its genesis to our need to explore the unexplained—as does every great work of art or music or literature. We are drawn powerfully to that which we don't fully understand, whether it is the mystery of the numinous, or secrets of the earth or of the stars and planets—or the secrets reflected in the eyes of a little cat.

Surely the cats' secrets have stirred the imaginations of writers.

One can't count the writers, contemporary or long dead, from Sue Grafton to Nancy Willard and Alice Adams to Ernest Hemingway, or Colette, whose homes and studios have been peopled with cats.

The writer's cat, prowling the desk and bookshelves, might hint of mysterious threads of story to untangle, or nuanced facets of character to sort out. Or perhaps the sly wit of the writer's cat is reflected in a body of work.

But the writer's cat is a healer, too, bringing to the often lonely workplace an oasis of warmth and comfort, a companionship that is welcome when work has gone awry or when one feels bleak and alone.

Whatever the cat's gifts to any of us, it is, of all the living creatures put on this earth by the *master* of mystery, perhaps the most elusive.

Surely, when we mix the mystery of cat with the mystery of Christmas, we call forth, as if by true magic, the voices of the storytellers. . . .

Renie Burghardt brings us tears as we experience her painful childhood in war-torn Hungary, with her beloved companion Paprika; but she offers us a gentle continuity, too, a sense of far more seen in this world than our immediate danger or pain. Steve Dale shows us how to love a very special and talented cat; we shed tears for Ricky, but we rejoice as Steve builds, to Ricky's memory, a most important monument. James Herriot's story of Buster is heartrending, too, yet it is filled with joy that brings happy tears at Christmas.

There are offerings that make us laugh and nod and say, "Having a new kitten *is* like that. I know exactly, Amy Shojai, what you are talking about." Or, after reading about Spit McGee, you might tell Willie Morris, I, too, have felt like this about cats—and I have reacted just as you did! In these pages we can live with Cleveland Amory as he discovers his own Christmas surprise. And we cry with Janine Adams at Spooky's disappearance, for the loss of a cat is devastating to a child—but his return is indeed a miracle.

If you are among the readers who like a touch of crime

for Christmas, Miriam Fields-Babineau's Christmas dinner may be in order. Or perhaps Rita Mae Brown's cat, Mrs. Murphy. Or Carole Nelson Douglas's brash and cheeky Midnight Louie. Or if you prefer to follow in the pawprints of the criminal himself—in this case, a feline hood of sophisticated talents—Jim Edgar's Vincent should please you. They're all here to entertain you, the storytellers and their cats. My own Christmas offering does not star Joe Grey, P.I., solving crimes along the California coast. This story is set in rural Georgia, as are others of my short stories. I did confer with Joe Grey on the matter of its inclusion; he has rendered his approval.

Both Betsy Stowe's poem and Laurie Loughlin's offer a happy touch of Christmas humor. Christine Church tenders help in keeping our cats safe during the holidays when we are apt to forget the dangers that the bustle and unusual foods and decorations present for them, particularly for lively kittens.

And with deep insight, both Beth Adelman and Wendy Christensen offer perceptive views of what *cats*, and *Christmas*, are really all about. Adelman asks, *Can* your cat speak to you? Which is something most true cat lovers wish their soft-pawed pals could do. And she shows how our cats do indeed communicate with us—or try to, if we will only pay attention.

Then, Wendy Christensen reminds us to strip away the stress and sham that the holidays embody for some of us. She shows us ". . . the antidote to the ritual madness that modern Christmas has become . . . The answer is right in front of us, dozing and purring on the window ledge in the sunshine." Wendy's wisdom eases away my own Christmas stress and returns me to the unencumbered joy I knew as a child.

We hope you will find, in this offering, a satisfying companion as you curl up before the fire with your own cats. And so, indeed, let the stories begin. . . .

Holiday Sparkles, or Home for the Holidays

Amy D. Shojai

rash-galumph-galumph-skiiiiiiid-*thump*!

"Amy! Will you please get *your cat* before she tears up the house?"

I sighed, and pushed away from the computer. My husband grew up catless. Mahmoud neither understood nor appreciated kitten antics, especially while he watched television sports.

Crash-galumph-galumph-skiiiiiiid-*thump*!

"Ameeeeeeee!"

By the sound of it, the eight-month-old delinquent had donned virtual racing stripes. She ran laps that traversed the carpeted living room and family room, slid across the oak floor entry, bumped down steps to the dining room, then finished with a claw-scrabbling turn around the slate-tiled kitchen.

Thumpa-thumpata-thumpa-THUMP!

Aha, a new path discovered. . . . The sound grew louder as she raced toward me up the stairs and flew down the hallway to land tippy-toed on the guest bed across the hall from my office. I peeked inside.

Seren(dipity) stared back with blue-jean-colored eyes. Then she self-inflated in mock terror and began trampoline calisthenics (*boing-boing-boing*) on the mattress.

I quickly shut the door, confining the demon seed— my husband's name for her—to my upstairs domain.

Back in June, a friend discovered the dumped kitten napping in an empty flowerpot on the back porch and called me, her pet-writer buddy, for help. I had been petless for longer than I cared to admit. E-mail, phone, and fax lines kept me connected to my clients and colleagues, but I figured the kitten would brighten the long, sometimes lonely workdays. Besides, as a pet writer I *needed* a pet. So it was *Amy-to-the-rescue*, and love at first sight.

My husband wasn't so easily smitten. He still missed our elderly and sedate German shepherd but cherished the freedom of being petless. I convinced him a lap-snuggling kitten would be no trouble. Besides, the cream-colored carpet he'd chosen matched the color of Seren's fur. It had to be an omen.

The cat gods have a wicked sense of humor. They made me pay for that fib.

The Siamese wannabe had no off-switch. She talked nonstop and demanded the last word. She opened drawers and explored kitchen cabinets. She answered my office phone but never took messages. And she left legions of sparkle ball toys everywhere.

The colorful toys polka-dotted the stairs. You'd think a peacock threw up. The toys floated in the kitten's water bowl, swirled in the toilet, and bobbed in my coffee cup. And Seren hid sparkle balls everywhere to later stalk and paw-capture them from beneath household appliances.

Mahmoud quickly learned to check his shoes each morning before putting them on. He was not amused. I knew better than to suggest he should be grateful Seren only stuffed his shoes with sparkle balls and not—ahem—other items.

I'd managed to buffer the cat-shock effect over the past months by keeping her in my office during the day and wearing Seren out with lots of games before Mahmoud came home from work. Weekends proved a challenge. By Monday morning, my husband reached his kitty threshold and welcomed a return to the cat-free zone at work.

But now the holidays loomed. Mahmoud looked forward to two weeks at home, two weeks of relaxation, two weeks of napping on the couch in front of the TV.

Two weeks of sharing the house with "the devil."

It would indeed be a Christmas miracle if we survived with sense of humor intact.

In the past we'd often visited my folks over the holidays, where we enjoyed a traditional snowy Indiana Christmas morning, stocking stuffers, decorated tree, lots of relatives, and a sumptuous turkey dinner. This year we planned a quiet celebration at home in Texas, so snow wasn't an option. But I wanted to decorate with lots of holiday sparkles to make the season as festive as possible.

"A Christmas tree? Don't cats *climb* trees?" Mahmoud's *you-must-be-insane* expression spoke volumes. He'd already blamed Seren for dumping his coffee on the cream-colored carpet. Maybe matching fur color wasn't such a great omen after all.

But 'tis the season of peace on earth, and I wanted to keep the peace—and the cat. So I agreed. No tree.

Mahmoud didn't particularly care if we decorated at all since Christmas isn't a part of his cultural or religious tradition. But he knew I treasured everything about the holidays. So we compromised.

Gold garlands with red velvet poinsettias festooned the curving staircase, wrapping around and around the banisters and handrail. Gold beads draped the fireplace mantel, with greeting cards propped above. A red cloth adorned the dining room table, while in the living room, the candelabra with twelve scented candles flickered brightly from inside the fireplace. Other candles in festive holders decorated the several end tables, countertops, and the piano.

The centerpiece of Christmas décor was the large glass-top coffee table placed midway between the fireplace, TV, and the leather sofa. The wooden table base carried puppy teeth marks, silent reminders of the dog Mahmoud and I still mourned. Since we had no tree, the table served to display brightly wrapped packages that fit underneath out of the way. And on top of the table I placed Grandma's lovely three-piece china nativity of Mary, Joseph, and the Baby in the manger.

Grandma died several years before, right after the holidays. Each family member was encouraged to request something of hers to keep as a special remembrance, and I treasured Grandma's nativity. The simple figurines represented not only the Holy Family but evoked the very essence of Grandma and every happy family holiday memory.

Of course, Seren created her own memories and put her paw into everything. It became her purpose in life to un-festoon the house. She "disappeared" three of the faux poinsettias, risked singed whiskers by sniffing candles, and stole bows off packages.

She decided the red tablecloth set off her feline beauty. She lounged in the middle of the table beneath the Tiffany-style shade that doubled as a heat lamp, shedding tiny hairs onto the fabric. As every cat lover eventually learns, fur is a condiment. But Mahmoud had not yet joined the cat-lover ranks and was not amused.

"Off! Get off the table. Amy, she'll break your glass lampshade."

*Crash-galumph-galumph-*skiiiiiiid-*thump*!

Mahmoud had no sooner resettled onto the sofa to watch the TV when the whirling dervish hit again. The twinkling gold beads dangling from the mantel caught her predatory attention. Seren stalked them from below, quickly realized she couldn't leap that high, and settled for pouncing onto the top of the TV. From there, only a short hop separated her from the ferocious mantel quarry she'd targeted.

"Off! Get off the TV. Amy, will you come get *your cat*?"

Crash-galumph-galumph-skiiiiiiid-*thump*!

I arrived in time to see her complete a second Mario Andretti lap. I swear she grinned at us as she skidded past. With the next drive-by Seren stopped long enough to grab my ankle, execute a ten-second feline headstand while bunny-kicking my calves, then resumed her mad dash around the house.

Mahmoud glared. "I thought you said cats sleep sixteen hours a day."

I shrugged and hid a smile. Seren had already learned what buttons to push. Rattling the wooden window blinds worked extremely well, but now she need only eye the decorations to garner all the attention she craved.

Cute kitty. Smart kitty. Mahmoud wasn't amused, but I was.

She raced into the living room, leaped onto the glass-top table, and belly-flopped alongside my treasured Holy Family. . . .

"Off! Get off." Mahmoud shooed the kitten out of the danger zone before I could react in shock. This time, I was not amused.

Mahmoud knew what Grandma's nativity meant to me. "Decorating was your idea. Don't blame me if the devil breaks something," he warned.

Before he could suggest it, I caught the miscreant and gave her a time-out in the laundry room to cool her jets. We'd relegated Seren's potty, food bowls, and bed to this room and routinely confined her at night or when away. Otherwise, she set off motion detectors and the house alarm—or dismantled the house while we slept. Besides, Mahmoud complained that Seren's purring kept him awake at night.

I used a wooden yardstick to fish toys from beneath the washer/dryer to provide necessary feline entertainment during the incarceration. Several dozen sparkle balls—red, orange, yellow, green, blue, pink, purple—and the three missing faux poinsettias emerged, along with an assortment of dust bunnies and dryer lint.

I sighed. The kitten's age meant several more

months of madcap activity, and I wasn't sure how much more Mahmoud could take. He only saw Seren at full throttle. He also suffered from "Saint Spot Syndrome," which meant he recalled only the happy memories of our beloved dog, and overlooked potty accidents, chewed shoes, and other normal canine misbehaviors of the past.

Seren suffered mightily in the comparison.

I felt exhausted after the first week of running vacation interference between my husband and the kitten. Whenever possible I kept Seren confined with me in my upstairs office but that backfired. She slept in my office, but once downstairs she turned into a dynamo intent on pick-pick-picking at Mahmoud, especially when he ignored her.

The second week began, and as Christmas drew near I found more and more errands that required my attention outside of the house. Mahmoud came with me for some, but other times he preferred TV.

"Just lock up the devil before you leave so she doesn't bother me," he said. "I don't want to watch her."

It made me nervous to leave them alone together in the house. I worried that Seren might commit some last-straw infraction and I'd be unable to salvage any potential relationship. I loved her, heaven help me; she'd hooked her claws deep into my heart. And I loved Mahmoud. I wanted my two loves to at least put up with each other.

But as I prepared to leave I couldn't find her. At less than five pounds, Seren could hide in the tiniest spaces. One time I found her inside the box springs of the guest bed, but that day—December 23rd—she disappeared and refused to come out of hiding.

I think she planned it. Maybe the spirit of the holidays inspired her. Or perhaps some other loving canine (or grandmotherly) influence worked its Christmas magic. Whatever the motivation, when I returned home that rainy December evening, my unspoken holiday wish had been granted.

I found my husband napping on the sofa. On the glass-top table beside him the Holy Family nested in a radiance of sparkle balls—an inspired feline gift of toys for a very special Child.

And atop Mahmoud's chest, quiet at last, rested a very happy kitten.

Mahmoud roused enough to open one eye. "Fafnir—

I mean *Seren* still purrs too loud," he grumbled.

Fafnir had been the name of our dog.

With a nod toward the overcast day Mahmoud added, "At least *our cat* won't need to be walked in the rain."

Seren blinked blue-jean-colored eyes and purred louder.

Along Comes Spit McGee from *My Cat Spit McGee*

WILLIE MORRIS

*I*t was Christmas in Dixie, still months before our wedding. My future stepson Graham was then in high school and had a girlfriend named Savannah. Savannah was cruising along old Highway 51 north of Jackson one afternoon when she sighted a little starving, abandoned kitten in a ditch. She got out and put her in the car and took her home. When Graham saw the kitten, he suggested Savannah let him give it to his mother for a Christmas surprise. She liked the idea. Neither of them checked this out with me, I can tell you.

Graham and his mother dwelled at the time in a house on Northside Drive in Jackson in a neighborhood built up right after World War II, so that all the side streets were named after war sites. This house was at the intersection of Northside and Normandy, a homey domicile with rambling rooms and a big fireplace and a good back porch and lawn. The three of us had decorated a tall fresh Mississippi cedar with old family angels and Santas and reindeer and lights, which twinkled from the pungent branches.

It was late on Christmas Eve. We were sitting in the room near the tree, with a substantial number of presents around it. Nat King Cole's "I'll Be Home for Christmas" was on the stereo, or maybe it was Bing Crosby's "O Come All Ye Faithful." Suddenly, as if on cue, there was an odd rustling from the rear of the tree. And then tentatively stepping out over the packages into view was a tiny pure-white kitten with a red Yuletide ribbon around its neck.

"How did *he* get in here?" I heard myself exclaiming.

"It's a *she*," Graham said. "It's for you, Mom."

The kitten looked a little intimidated, which was precisely the way *I* felt in that moment. Although Savannah and Graham had fed and bathed her, she was a scrawny thing. But when my future spouse saw her, her features became flushed and joyous. Never had I seen such a happy female. She immediately swept the creature into her arms and embraced her. Then the kitten jumped onto the floor, ran back under the tree, and immediately shimmied up the main trunk. Christmas balls and angels crashed to the floor. Cedar trees are very dense, especially those strung with lights and ornaments. There was no way to coax her down; she would only climb farther up the tree. She was obviously going to come down when she was good and damned ready. "Just don't pay any attention to her and she'll come down sooner or later," JoAnne instructed. So we didn't, and that is precisely what she did.

It was a critical moment in my life, and by God I knew it. I left the room with the cat still in the tree and went outside to get some air. Only a couple of days before I had seen on TV a movie about one of my boyhood World War II heroes, Admiral "Bull" Halsey, who when asked about his fluctuating strategies during the Battle of Guadalcanal replied, "It's not so much that you change your mind as that you go in a different direction." Well, it *was* Christmas, after all. I promised myself to at least give it a civilized try. I took a deep breath and went back inside.

On Christmas morning the little kitten was lapping milk from a bowl on the floor. She turned and looked at me, and I looked back at her. It was the genesis of a most unfamiliar relationship. Of course I did not know it then, but she would someday be the mother of Spit McGee.

The Cat Woman said she would allow me to name the kitten. I knew this was a craven bribe, but I named her Rivers Applewhite after the little girl I grew up with and wrote about, the one that Old Skip and I were both in love with. Perhaps the name itself would help me tolerate the unwarranted Christmas cat.

So now we had a Rivers Applewhite. She was an enigma to me. She was, as I have reported, absolutely white, with singular dark brown eyes. She was also very resilient and temperamental, and in her early days in that house kept testing me, as if I were unworthy of her. I tried not to pay her much mind, but she kept doing exasperating things that I was unable to ignore. She would perch silently on the rafters of the den, for example, then without warning leap down at me and land next to me on the sofa, thus scaring me witless. Mostly she would just sit and stare at me with her cantankerous, knowing eyes. What did she *know*? I certainly had no idea. She was exceedingly fast, and sometimes out of whatever motive she mindlessly sprinted through the dwelling with the velocity of a Jackie Joyner-Kersee. She was always hiding. The house was not of San Simeon proportions, but her hiding places were multifold and uncanny: under the kitchen sink, all the chairs and sofas and beds, in my shoes, and once even in the fireplace when it was not in use—what that did to a white cat is easy to imagine—and on the wall-length bookshelves. One day, after being missing for a couple of hours, we discovered her wedged between *The Brothers Karamazov* and *Down and Out in Paris and London*. As part of the Cat Woman's later confessional, she said: "Since she was a Christmas surprise, I didn't have an opportunity to think about how you'd react to her. And I'll bet neither did you. And how could I disappoint Graham and Savannah? I simply had to figure out a way to work her into our relationship and hope you'd go along with it. I never considered that you wouldn't."

Rivers obviously was drawn to my fiancée but mainly treated me on the scale of a ratty indentured servant just off steerage from eighteenth-century Liverpool. To put it mildly, I did not trust her very much, even on those winter nights she spent drowsily in front of the fireplace, tame as could be.

The first real test came a week or so after Christmas and was a trying one. We had enlisted my other future stepson, Gibson, to help me move out of my bungalow at Ole Miss and to bring all my possessions back to Jackson. The Cat

Woman insisted we take Rivers Applewhite with us. She did not like it one bit. It was a three-hour drive to Oxford, and she whined and screamed and walked every inch of the car and on the car seats and under the car seats and on our necks. Once between Coffeeville and Water Valley she jumped onto my head and almost caused me to lose control of my clanking Dodge. "That cat is driving me crazy!" I shouted. I suggested we stop at a pharmacy and get her a high-powered sedative, something that would knock her out cold, or for that matter forever. But somehow she finally settled down and we made it to our destination.

Once we arrived at my old place on Faculty Row, she was completely at home. Against all odds she immediately began to conduct herself with an unexpected decency. She took a place on the back of my big sofa and spent the next few days gazing out the window at the happenings on the street outside. The spirit of my noble departed Labrador, Pete, pervaded the house: the corners where he slumbered, his own personal woolen carpet in front of the fireplace, the spot in the dining room where he reclined as I wrote my stories. At any moment I expected him to come in the back door and leap up at me and lick my nose, then explore his familiar territory until against all reasonable justice he discovered a *cat* on his old premises. That might have sent him back to his grave. I was consumed with guilt when I used Pete's old food platter to put down cat food. It is always melancholy to move away forever from a place where you have dwelled for a very long time, for the past accumulates on you in fading mementos, documents and letters and photographs, reminders of the mortal days, and it is particularly trying to gather up these haunting artifacts of temporality with a cat looking at you. *What have I gotten myself into, Pete?*

I had to concede that Rivers was very smart. She could figure things out by herself. She soon determined that I did not have a clue about how to deal with her. I guess I just treated her as if she were a dog in cat's clothing, giving her sturdy slaps of affection, from which she would promptly run away. When I dumped whole cans of cat food onto her dish she would take a bite or two and contemptuously walk off. I saved huge hunks of meat and bones from my plate and put them down for her, and some sliced bologna—had not my dog Skip liked bologna?—and she ignored them all. She would not come when I called her or clapped my hands vigorously to get her attention or beat on the sofa for her to sit beside me. When I picked her up, she would not stay with me. Why could she not at least show even the most modest indications that she was happy to see me and to greet me when I was gone for several days? This puzzled and angered me. "Cats ain't dogs," I would shout accusingly at the Cat Woman.

This cat seemed basically a maverick, a loner, as I had always judged cats to be. There was a haughtiness to her, a demeanor of aristocracy that contradicted her incontrovertible Highway 51 ancestry. As she began to grow up, I also had to admit that she was pretty. She was an immaculate self-groomer and would spend interminable moments licking her paws and fur and tail. She was strange. Sometimes to see her reaction I would call out her name. Most of the time she would sit there disregarding me, but every now and again she would turn and acknowledge my call with lazy, dreamy eyes—ennui eyes: *What do you want?*

Nonetheless, as I watched Rivers grow into a graceful, elegant young cat, I began to suspect she was more deep and subtle than I had supposed. I read at the Cat Woman's urging the exotic fairy tale "The White Cat," which the Mississippi artist Walter Anderson had interpreted in splendid block prints and which my friend Ellen Douglas had retold in her book *The Magic Carpet and Other Tales*. Despite her detached ways, Rivers could have been the magical cat princess whom the king's youngest son fell in love with.

She had the instincts of the huntress, as I had indeed been forewarned about cats, and warily stalked our backyard on stealthy paws seeking things out. Sometimes she sharpened her claws on the bark of trees. I watched from afar as she scooted up these trees to their remotest branches, as if she were practicing what to do if something came after her. No one was teaching her these things; she just did them. The first time she came in the house with a lizard in her mouth, I was tempted to contact the lizard department of the humane society. This was a vicinity of squirrels, and she chased them incessantly with no success.

Since she was being well fed, she was fattening up and growing. One night something unforeseen happened. I was sitting in a chair reading a book when she suddenly leapt into my lap and began purring. She extended her paws and kneaded them on my legs. She began licking my fingers, surprising me not only by the intimacy of her action but by the sharp-razor feel of her tiny tongue. Did she think I was her *mother*? Or was she flirting with me? This was a new experience, a cat sitting in *my* lap and purring at *me*. Was something happening to me? We lived in a neighborhood with yards and trees, where cats could be indoors and outdoors. I began to worry that on her explorations outside the house she might get run over. I discovered myself standing on the back porch waiting for her to return.

Beyond a certain age a kitten grows up quickly. The following April, we noticed that her stomach was beginning to bulge. Surely she was not *pregnant*; she was still just a kitten, only five or six months old. I could hardly believe it: she was indeed with child. She would be a child mother, or at best a teenaged mother. "White trash!" I yelled at her.

Her conduct and demeanor now affected me, however. She became more affectionate toward me. There was a vulnerability to her, a warmth that I had never thought possible with cats. Could this have been an old, atavistic association with time itself? One afternoon I gazed at her for the longest moments as she rested on an ironing board on the back porch in the bedappled sunshine. Her tiny leonine eyes were aglow: she was *expecting* something. Occasionally she would awaken and gently lick her burgeoning belly. At other times I observed her as she searched the house for more secretive places to sleep.

The days went by. We were now well into May, in the flowering of the great Deep Southern springtime.

We knew Rivers's childbirth was imminent but did not know precisely when it would be. I found myself a little worried about this forthcoming event. This bizarre little cat had somehow, despite my reluctance, become at least an oblique part of my life, and I started quizzing JoAnne about the mechanics of cat-birthing. The Cat Woman did not seem to give it a thought. Most of her life, she reminded me, she had had at least one mother cat who had kittens every year and that when the time came the cat always went off by herself somewhere—usually to a closet, sometimes under a bed or in an outside storage room—and had the kittens. The Cat Woman never knew precisely when to expect this and never did much in the way of preparation. This seemed a fairly cavalier attitude to me. All the dogs of my life had been males, so I had had no experience with dog births, either. With her previous cats JoAnne used to just put some old towels or sheets or T-shirts in a little flat box in a small area in the back of a closet and show it to the expectant mother. If the cat liked the spot she would use that as her birthing bed, but if this did not suit her she would find her own space and make her own bed. She tried to explain that Rivers Applewhite would know instinctively what to do, but I was not convinced. "She's too young," I said, "not even a teenager yet." So we made places in every closet and dark nook and under every bed. The Mayo Clinic could not have done better.

As the delivery date approached David Rae was visiting from Minneapolis and we had a dinner party for him and some of his Jackson friends. Everyone was petting Rivers and predicting when she would deliver. The group left around midnight. Shortly after that, catastrophic things began to transpire.

This would become one of the memorable happenings of my life. I was sitting at the dining room table while JoAnne cleared the dishes. Suddenly Rivers began moaning and crying and running inanely from room to room. We tried to calm her down, but she refused to be pacified. One moment she would hide under a bed, the next in one of the closets. Every five minutes or so she would repeat the routine. This went on time and again. I was already a nervous wreck. How had I gotten into this? JoAnne decided something was badly wrong and telephoned the all-night emergency animal clinic. As I trailed Rivers in her frenetic scrambles, I could hear

JoAnne describing what was going on and asking if a cat ever needed a cesarean or if she might not instinctively know how to give birth. The emergency vet said both were possible but to give her more time before we brought her in.

Soon after the phone call, Rivers started her dervish again. But this time as I followed her dashing from the bedroom closet into the dining room she did something that nothing whatever in my entire existence had remotely prepared me for. She flung from her insides onto the floor a slimy gray thing with no head or eyes or nose or ears or tail! "Oh, my God!" JoAnne shouted. "She's had a deformed baby! Or maybe it's premature?" Rivers lurched nearby as I squeamishly hovered over the formless blob, which resembled nothing if not the pulsating pods in the old movie *Invasion of the Body Snatchers*. Once again JoAnne phoned the emergency vet and described the situation. He calmly suggested that perhaps the amniotic sac was still in place on the newly born kitten. He proceeded to give her exact directions on what to do. With the telephone cord pulled out to its fullest length, she began relaying the instructions to me.

Indulge me, reader, to interject here that when I was growing up, people expected me to be a medical doctor— that was what all bright Southern boys were supposed to aspire to then, but I would not for a nonce so much as think of it, and for one very sound reason: I hated the sight of blood. And here I was at 2 A.M. in a house in Jackson, Mississippi, expected to deliver a cat. "I don't know nothin' about birthin' cats," I heard myself saying. But there was scant choice.

"Get some paper towels," the vet's orders were repeated to me. "Rub the thing up and down and over and over." I proceeded to do so. After a minute or more of this, beneath the oozing blood I began to see ears and a nose and a head—a little cat, a little *white* cat.

"Continue rubbing! This is what the mother should be doing by licking the kitten!" So I rubbed and rubbed.

"Rub it hard on the back to help it breathe! *Pat! Pat!*" This went on endlessly. "Live, kid, live!" I yelled. And, by God, it began breathing deeply and making faint noises and moving its mouth.

Somehow all of this seemed to calm Rivers Applewhite, and she sedately retreated into the bedroom closet again and gave birth to another one—a yellow one. She did everything right this time. I took the little white one in my arms and gently put it in there with her. Then she delivered another white one and a little black-and-white one all by herself.

I would give the first little white one, whose life I had saved, the name Spit McGee.

The name derived from a character in a children's book I once wrote. Spit was a mischievous and resourceful boy who could spit farther than anyone else in the whole town. This is how I described him in that book:

Spit lived in the swamps, and he was a hunter and fisherman. Foxie Topkins might bring an apple to school for the teacher, but not Spit. If he brought her anything it would be a catfish, or a dead squirrel for frying. Rivers Applewhite would often be the recipient of the most beautiful wild swamp flowers, which Spit brought into town in the spring. One day during recess Spit reached into his pockets and pulled out a dead grubworm, a live boll weevil, a wad of chewed-up bubble gum, four leaves of poison ivy which he said he was not allergic to, two shotgun shells, a small turtle, a rusty fish hook, the feather from a wild turkey, a minnow, the shrunken head of a chipmunk, and a slice of bacon.

And with his namesake begins a new chapter in this vainglorious writer's life.

Without wishing to sound histrionic, the birth of Spit and his three siblings evoked for me a reserve of continuity, of the generations, of life passing on life, of the cycles. By the second day it was obvious that Rivers, so poignantly and recently a kitten herself, was making a good little mother, her maternal instincts as strong as those of the backyard huntress.

Although the kittens' eyes would remain closed for ten days or so, when they were only hours old they were active and curious. The white female kitten we named Savannah, after my stepson's girlfriend who had rescued Rivers from the ditch on Highway 51. She looked bigger and healthier than Spit. We named the yellow one Peewee after a childhood chum of mine, and the black-and-white one Jimmy Carter for regional reasons. Any good mother loves and fears for her young, and I noted how Rivers would take the kittens with her mouth around the backs of their necks and hide them somewhere from time to time, as if she felt incipient dangers lurking for them. Once she had them settled somewhere, she was almost like a generic time clock. She would nurse them and watch over them, and about every two and a half hours as they slept together in a furry mass she would emerge to eat, relax, lie outside in the sunshine—then soon metronomically return to them again.

Then we discovered that Rivers and the kittens had fleas. This turned out to be a wicked flea year in Jackson, which happens every now and then, and the kittens had more than their share. JoAnne called the vet for information about what to do. Just powder them with another kind of flea powder, the vet advised, and gave a brand name. So we began bringing the kittens out one by one and lavishing them with flea powder. Each time we did this, Rivers would move the kittens to another hiding place. After three or four of these moves, she located a spot we could not find. For days we would see her sneak through a cabinet in the basement, but search as we did we could not locate the sequestered kittens. She began spending more time away from them, and we became anguished. Friends came and helped us look, but the kittens had vanished.

Finally, we found her hiding place under the house. I crawled under there and looked at them. Only one of the kittens was alive—one of the white ones. I surmised it was Savannah, since little Spit had been so tiny to begin with. But she was alive just barely, only a wisp of life lingering, as if she would expire at any moment. I put her in my arms and we took her to the car to rush her to the animal emergency clinic.

JoAnne drove the three miles to the clinic. To allow the stricken kitten to breathe better, I held her up on the dashboard. She was only slightly bigger than the palm of my hand. She hardly could move there. But she extended her paws toward me, as if she desperately wanted to live, bobbing her head lightly back and forth. At the destination JoAnne was too distraught to leave the car. I took the kitten inside.

The animal nurse on duty examined the patient and declared her technically dead. Nothing could be done, she said. But then the veterinarian came in, whose name was Dr. Majure. He looked over the woebegone little creature more closely. "There's hope," he said. "We've got a cat who gives blood transfusions to sick kittens." They called him Clinic Cat and he had already saved several kittens. He was two years old, weighed sixteen pounds, and had Type B blood, he said, the preferred type for cat transfusions.

"Your kitten's dying of anemia. Leave him here overnight. We'll fetch Clinic Cat. There's a chance we can save him. I can't promise. Come back in the morning."

I was about to leave, but tarried at the door. "Did I

hear you say *him*? My cat?"

"Sure. He's a male."

In the car I told JoAnne about the projected transfusion, then: "But it's not Savannah. It's Spit McGee."

I spent a restless night, consumed with worry for the dying Spit. With trepidation I returned the next day. The vet brought him out to me. "He's going to be okay. The little fellow didn't want to die." The transformation from the previous night was miraculous. His eyes were bright and he moved about vigorously in the arms of the vet. "This is going to be a good cat, this boy," he surmised. "This is going to be a *bad* cat. See what I've noticed? He's got one blue eye and one golden eye. That's a good sign. And look who's here." A huge, furry cat with Siamese eyes and eclectic orange colors strolled into the room. I knew who this was without asking. "Thank you, Clinic Cat," I said.

Vincent

JIM EDGAR

he Christmas light displays along Tacoma's Division Avenue formed the same configurations as last year, and the year before that. It was this consistency that made Vincent smile as he walked along the sidewalk admiring the various spectacles. On one lawn, brilliant diamonds formed reindeer and snowmen, while the house next door was a flashing kaleidoscopic nightmare. It's enough to give a cat a seizure, Vincent thought.

He trotted down the street to a house adorned with twinkling icicles. A year earlier, he had been standing in the same spot watching a white female kitten jumping along the sill of the house's large front window. The window's curtain was closed this year.

The velvet satchel that hung around Vincent's neck was growing heavy, its contents demanding delivery. It can wait, he thought. Christmas only comes once a year.

A soft glow exuded from the side of the house. Vincent crept across the lawn and followed the light to a low window. He jumped to the sill and peered in. The same family as last year; mother, father, son. The boy had grown quite a bit. How old was he now . . . six perhaps? More handsome, a bit more blond. Vincent imagined the boy playing with the kitten, giving her treats, stroking her back, opening her Christmas presents for her. The boy giggled and climbed to his father's lap on a large recliner. Vincent sighed and let his gaze wander, searching for the white kitten.

Around the far corner of the living room she came at full speed, dodging the coffee table and barely missing the bounty of gifts piled beneath the family Christmas tree. She slipped on the linoleum of the dining area and disappeared around another corner. Vincent waited for her return from the other room, wondering which gifts were hers. Finally, when she didn't appear, he jumped from the sill and crept back to the sidewalk.

He turned to look back down Division Avenue. Lights as far as he could see. Lights on houses, houses with families, some families with cats. But none of the houses were his and none of the families were his. Vincent stood alone and watched the lights blaze.

He walked away to make his delivery.

Three blocks away, Vincent was still enchanted by the Christmas lights when he was surprised by Sammy of Hilltop. So surprised that he struck out at Sammy with a six-clawed right hook.

"Hey, Vinnie, it's me!" Sammy cried, barely avoiding the potentially lethal swipe.

"Sorry, Sammy! You surprised me! You should know better."

Sammy was catching his breath as he spoke. "Rolfondo told me to find you, in a hurry too. He needs you to make one more pickup in Old Town."

Vincent sighed. Old Town Tacoma took him farther out of his way than he would have liked—all the way down to the original Tacoma waterfront. He only wanted to drop off his collection sack and go home to be with his solitary thoughts.

"The Phuong brothers?" Vincent asked, annoyed that the reverie of his evening would likely be marred by violence.

"Yeah. He said you know them best, so you'd have more luck."

Vincent nodded. When the brothers first arrived in Tacoma, the eldest, True, had struck out on his own, finding employment with Vincent's boss as an enforcer.

More muscle than brains, True had looked to Vincent for help more than once on assignments and had even shared Vincent's home for a year. Rolfondo, Vincent's boss, had finally had enough and sent True back to his own family.

"How much do they owe?"

"Dunno, probably a lot. They haven't paid anything yet."

"Okay," Vincent reluctantly agreed. "Can you do me a favor and take this back to Rolfondo for me?" he asked, motioning to the satchel hanging from his neck.

"Oh no, Vinnie. You know how that stuff messes me up," Sammy said.

Vincent knew. He had seen Sammy flip out over lesser quality catnip before. The thought of taking an almost-full sack into Old Town made him nervous, but losing it all to Sammy's instinctual feline reactions would be unforgivable. Their boss didn't accept such lack in judgment.

"Okay," Vincent said. "Tell Rolfondo I will see him in an hour."

The waterfront was fifteen minutes away, at a good clip, and from there only half an hour to the warehouse. This gave Vincent some extra time to check out the light displays on the boats docked along the old piers. They always brought cheer to his loneliest time of the year.

"Alright, Vinnie. See you later." Sammy turned and trotted down the street.

"Hey, Sammy. Merry Christmas."

"Yeah," Sammy said over his shoulder. "You too, Vinnie."

Vincent sighed. He had yet to have a merry Christmas.

On his way to the Old Town, Vincent noticed the houses along the way. A few were draped with colored strings of lights, some flickering, some not. None of them approached the grandiosity of Division Avenue, but they evoked emotions nevertheless. He thought back to his first Christmas five years earlier.

He was only a few months old, and living with a carcass of a man who made his way in life as a personal injury attorney. The man had decided, in a drunken rage, to visit an opposing counselor and took Vincent along for the ride. While the attorney spent most of the night cursing the man from outside his house, Vincent sat in the car watching the

Christmas lights along the street flash on and off. When they arrived home, Vincent was left, forgotten, in the backseat of the car amid legal briefs and empty beer bottles. Finally the man returned for him, but not before Vincent had had an accident on the floor of the car.

Vincent recalled the rest of that night with a shudder. No one should have to spend their first Christmas alive like that. And the next two years were not much better. The lawyer became increasingly violent as his life deteriorated from alcohol abuse. Often finding himself at the business end of a counterfeit Bruno Magli, Vincent developed quick reflexes, but he never raised a polydactyl paw against the man. Through all the injustices suffered at his hands, Vincent still felt pity for him. But not enough to stick around forever.

The best day of my life, Vincent thought, was squeezing through that barely open window and leaving the drunk to die miserable and alone. He looked at the lights twinkling in front of him now and put the memory behind him. The first three years of his life were barely worth remembering. They were not without merit, though. Without all the drunken abuse, I would not be the street-wise, tough guy I am now, would I? Vincent thought. But do I really need to be a tough guy? All I ever really wanted was a warm place to sleep and a family . . . a family that doesn't kick me around the room for fun.

That's not too much to ask for, is it? Vincent wondered, looking up into the dark sky above.

Vincent looked both ways and crossed Ruston Way, arriving at the old Tacoma waterfront. He meandered between the bustling alehouses that now lined the shore to the kluges of rotting pier pilings, remnants of Tacoma's golden days as a proud port city. Carefully, he crawled down to the craggy rocks among the pilings, rocks that had claimed the lives of too many cats. Slimy stone and frigid tides were not a feline's best friend.

Still, he liked coming here when business was not involved. He remembered the stories he had heard of the old neighborhood, full of colorful longshoremen unloading the freighters coming in from parts unknown. Now these old docks were the refuge of the occasional homeless person, or in this case, a rogue gang of fish-poaching Vietnamese felines.

It was these poachers, the Phuong brothers, to whom Vincent owed this late night visit. Vincent's boss, Rolfondo of Washington, had given them permission to intercept a small shipment of prawns destined for the Tacoma fish markets. They had turned a tidy profit on the job, but were very delinquent in paying Rolfondo his proper percentage. Weeks had passed, and it was time for Vincent to deliver a reminder. He had been doubly gifted at birth with immunity to catnip and with polydactylism: six claws on each paw. These gifts, combined with reflexive skills learned at the foot of the trial attorney, had earned him a title within the Tacoma family and the respect of cats as far south as Los Angeles. He was the only collector-enforcer in the family, capable of bringing in an ounce of 'nip at a time, impervious to its effect, an effect that made simpering blobs of lesser collectors.

This was Vincent's specialty. The three Phuong brothers had arrived from Vietnam on a container ship sailing under the flag of China. While True was testing the waters with Rolfondo's family, the other brothers started trading in foreign baubles and exotic fish. After True's return, they moved primarily into the catnip business and became one of the more notorious gangs in the city.

Amid the pier pilings Vincent now struggled through, they had found a secure niche at the base of a much-decayed concrete foundation and constructed an impressive fortress of some of the strongest crates in the business.

As he approached their enclave, Vincent gave his signature high-pitched warbling mewl, and waited. He watched carefully for any signs of movement. Though the brothers had recently become their own best customers, they were still dangerous. Personal history aside, True could still make trouble for Vincent.

A face appeared above one of the crates. Tran Phuong, the family deal-maker. Strictly business, Tran was the cat Vincent wanted to deal with.

"Ah, Vinnie the Craw!" Tran said, his accent mutilating Vincent's street name.

"Vincent of Tacoma, Tran." Vincent sighed. He had never liked his moniker, "The Claw," but it was tradition and held an air of respect.

"Okay, Vinnie. You don't come around to say Merry Christmas, yes?"

"No, Tran. I come to say you still owe for the prawn job. You are very overdue."

"Oh, payment, yes. Let me see here." Tran disappeared.

Vincent heard whispering and approached the fortress. The Phuong brothers didn't always play fair.

Lesser collectors had returned from their turf with scars to show for it. He crouched and peered inside.

Scattered about were twigs of pine, folded into absurd wreaths bound with soiled crimson ribbon and decorated with bottle caps. In the center of the place was an old cinderblock where two chipped sake cups sat, filled with cold tea.

A Vietnamese Christmas, Vincent thought. Good for them.

Another face appeared. Much larger than Tran, it was True.

"Hello, True," Vincent said pensively. "Is Loc in there with you too?"

"Loc? Oh yes, he is sleeping," True said smiling. "He is waiting for Santa Crause. You came for 'nip, Vinnie, but . . . we have none. You know how it is right now. We . . ."

Vincent interrupted him. "You guys have had five weeks. No 'nip in a month? C'mon, I know you better than that."

Tran popped up behind True. There was a slight daze in his eyes. His head rolled to one side as he looked at Vincent. He's high, Vincent thought. So much for no 'nip. At least he won't be much trouble.

"Vinnie," True said. "It *is* hard times. Not much 'nip

come by the old docks right now. Not even dirt weed. We promise, after New Year's, we pay up." Not in the mood to bargain, Vincent stretched, opening his claws wide, and looked at True. True's head hung lower, his eyes half-open. Holy Morris, Vincent thought, they are both high. Definitely not much trouble.

Vincent yowled and leapt at True, swiping a claw just above his head. True lifted a claw in defense, but was too late. Vincent's claw nicked True's ear, drawing blood. True whined from the attack.

Vincent landed behind Tran and easily pushed him aside with his forepaws. He faced True.

"Vinnie, please," True said staggering, "for old times sake."

And Vincent saw something in True's eyes. Something familiar. A silent request, almost desperate, for compassion and leniency.

Vincent shuddered. He knew that look; it was his own, many years ago. It was the same soft plea he had given the attorney years earlier, before being booted across the floor by the drunk.

Vincent sympathized with the emotion behind True's pitiful gaze. Why, he thought, should tonight be the same for the Phuong brothers as it was for me? Roughing these guys up, on Christmas Eve, of all nights. To what benefit? They are sitting down to have some cold tea and wait for Santa Crause and I have to screw it all up because they are too stupid or lazy to keep a couple grams of catnip out of their noses.

"You guys gotta pay up soon, you know," Vincent said.

"Vinnie, of course. I promise. I make it up to you."

How does the billboard go? Vincent thought. *You* can break the cycle.

"Okay, not tonight." He looked at their silly grins and smiled. "Merry Christmas, Phuong brothers."

Without the standard fare of abuse he usually meted out to delinquents, Vincent found himself with more than enough time to cruise the waterfront. He strolled over to the small cluster of boats that gathered by the old docks every Christmas season.

The boats were tied together by their owners and decked out with amazing arrays of holiday displays. Vincent's favorite was the low-end yacht that kept a menagerie of bejeweled reindeer on its bow. Then the two sailboats that hung a new Psalm, spelled out in flickering lights, between their masts every year. They must never get the presents they ask for, he thought.

He reached the end of the waterfront and headed south to the family headquarters, leaving the boats until next year.

There, in front of the entrance to Rolfondo's office, he saw two St. Petersburg hairless, the feline bodyguards of Samson of Washington, Rolfondo's boss and the head of the state family.

The Peterbalds nodded to him as he approached. "Vincent of Tacoma," they said.

"Alexsandr of Washington, Zhenya of Washington," he replied. He walked past them and scratched a sequence on the metal slab that blocked the entrance. From within the warehouse, the security door was pushed aside. He entered.

The room was rather empty, unusual for a family boss. But Rolfondo was a humble cat, more business than pleasure. He would be the first to tell you, "The more you have, the more you have to lose." And it showed in the simplicity of his official residence. Some pillows lay in the corner of the room, and in front of them, ornately carved ebony food bowls. On two of the pillows sat Rolfondo of Washington and Samson of Washington.

Between them, a slab of fresh salmon lay upon a silver tray. Rolfondo was nibbling at it as Vincent approached him.

"Vincent of Tacoma!" Samson said.

"Samson of Washington," Vincent replied, stretching on his front paws and lowering his head, acknowledging Samson's seniority. Samson smiled wide. He leaned forward and rubbed his nose on Vincent, a rare show of affection from the seventeen-year-old boss. But Samson knew Vincent's story and treated him as the son he never had.

"Thank you, sir," Vincent said.

"All the other cats are gone for the holiday," Samson said. "What are you doing here? Don't get me wrong, I am delighted to see you, my boy."

Rolfondo answered for Vincent. "I needed him to take care of those Vietnamese down by the old docks. They are too far behind for my liking." He looked at Vincent. "Well, what did you get from those three slack-a-bouts?"

"Well," Vincent started to reply. He looked at Samson and lowered his head, ashamed to show weakness. "They said they didn't have anything."

Rolfondo snorted. "And you believed that? Vincent, you know better than to trust a bunch of 'nip heads like . . ."

Vincent interrupted him. "No, sir. I didn't believe them. It's just that . . ."

"Just that what?" Rolfondo thundered. "You could

have sent them back to that shithole they call home with one paw tied behind your back!"

"Now, now," Samson said. "Let's hear what he has to say, Rolfondo."

"I have to say," Vincent paused. "I have to say that it is Christmas Evening, sirs. I know they were probably holding, and probably stoned at the time, but . . . I couldn't rough them up tonight. Not on Christmas, sirs. They don't have much to live for as it is. They only owe a few grams and . . ."

"Rolfondo, I think he's getting soft in his old age," Samson said, winking at Vincent, who winced at the accusation. He wasn't that old, and certainly wasn't getting soft. He knew Samson was being playful, but he regretted showing weakness in front of his elders.

"Perhaps so, Samson," Rolfondo replied. He looked at Vincent. "Do you have the other pickups?"

"Oh, yes, sir." Vincent pawed at the satchel hanging from his neck until it fell to the floor. He pushed it over to Rolfondo.

"Eh, get that away from me. You know how it messes me up," Rolfondo protested. Vincent swiped the sack into the corner of the room.

"Give the boy a break, Rolfondo," Samson said. "It is Christmas Eve. I know you have a heart somewhere in there." He poked at Rolfondo.

"Ah, I suppose so, Samson, I suppose so. Go on home, Vincent. You've done well as usual," Rolfondo said.

Vincent nodded to Samson and Rolfondo. "Merry Christmas, sirs."

Vincent's neighborhood was conspicuously devoid of Christmas festivity. His friends joked that it was the only all-Jewish area in Tacoma, but Vincent blamed the lack of decoration on the high number of elderly residents, too fragile to bother with the dangers of falling from ladders.

In the backyard of one elderly man, Vincent had made a home in an abandoned camping trailer. Too old to drive, the man paid no attention to it, except for a tarpaulin to keep the rain out.

Vincent hopped onto the top of the trailer and crawled under the tarp to the cracked skylight that was his door. He jumped to the table inside and over to the double bed at the rear of the trailer. There was the woolen blanket Rolfondo had given him on the day of his promotion to collector.

He pushed it into a pile and crawled beneath it. Within minutes he had put the day behind him and fell to sleep.

Christmas morning woke Vincent with a shiver. He climbed from his blanket and looked outside. Giant snowflakes were falling past the window. He purred and jumped to the skylight and pulled himself out.

A little slower than usual, he thought. I may need to find a place without such high ceilings. He jumped to the wall next to the trailer and down to the ground.

He pawed the frosty ground playfully, causing a spray of white behind him. Squeezing through a hole in the wooden fence, he went over to his favorite bush to pee.

A screech startled him.

"Come back here, cat!" a voice yelled.

He looked down the alley. A boy was running toward him. So was a cat. Vincent crouched, ready to spring over the fence and avoid the whole scene.

"Come back with my Christmas present!" the boy yelled. His voice was familiar to Vincent, and then he remembered. The kid lived around the corner with his mother.

When True and Vincent had roamed the neighborhood together, the boy had always tried to coax True into his house with pieces of fish. Vincent had felt jealous of the attention paid to True, but he had never mentioned it.

Now the boy was running toward him. But why was he chasing this cat?

Then Vincent recognized the cat. He was carrying something in his mouth as he bounded toward Vincent. Something the boy wanted back.

"True?" Vincent said, realizing it was the Phuong brothers' enforcer. "What are you doing here?"

True Phuong ran up to him and dropped something from his mouth. "Merry Christmas, Vinnie the Craw!" he said, smiling. Vincent looked at him, wondering if True was still high from the night before.

On the ground was an Army man action figure, new from the looks of it, except for a tooth mark or two.

"Is this for me?" Vincent asked, confused.

"Vinnie! Your Christmas wish is no secret to me. I told you I make it up to you," True said. He turned and ran down the alley past the boy, who was about to reach Vincent.

"Please, kitty, don't take my G.I. Joe, it's my Christmas present," the boy said.

Vincent looked at the toy on the ground. The boy approached slowly and crouched in front of Vincent. The knees of his pants were thinning, his pink skin starting to show through. He must be freezing, Vincent thought.

"I'm Fred," the boy said. His eyes were kind and inviting, his smile genuine. He reached out a hand. Vincent sat still and let Fred rub his head. The boy's touch was gentle. It reminded him of the kindness Samson showed with the rub of his nose. He arched his back and let Fred stroke him.

They sat together for what seemed an eternity, Fred rubbing and caressing Vincent's fur, forgetting about his toy soldier.

"You look cold. Do you want some warm milk?" Fred asked, breaking the reverie. Vincent replied with a long purr and rubbed against Fred's leg.

"I have to get home before Mom worries about me, but she won't mind if you have Christmas dinner with us." Fred stood and looked down at Vincent.

"Unless you have other plans," Fred said.

Vincent had no other plans.

"What a crazy cat, huh?" Fred said, picking up his G.I. Joe. He wiped it off and started walking down the alley.

Vincent took a step toward Fred and then looked back at his home. The trailer will still be there, he thought. And tail up, ears sharp, Vincent followed Fred home.

The Rescue
from *The Cat Who*
Came for Christmas

To anyone who has ever been owned by a cat, it will come as no surprise that there are all sorts of things about your cat you will never, as long as you live, forget.

Not the least of these is your first sight of him or her.

That my first sight of mine, however, would ever be memorable seemed, at the time, highly improbable. For one thing, I could hardly see him at all. It was snowing, and he was standing some distance from me in a New York City alley. For another thing, what I did see of him was extremely unprepossessing. He was thin and he was dirty and he was hurt.

The irony is that everything around him, except him, was beautiful. It was Christmas Eve, and although no one outside of New York would believe it on a bet or a Bible,

New York City can, when it puts its mind to it, be beautiful. And that Christmas Eve some years ago was one of those times.

The snow was an important part of it—not just the snow, but the fact it was still snowing, as it is supposed to but rarely does over Christmas. And the snow was beginning to blanket, as at least it does at first, a multitude of such everyday New York sins as dirt and noise and smells and potholes. Combined with this, the Christmas trees and the lights and decorations inside the windows, all of which can often seem so ordinary in so many other places, seemed, in New York that night, with the snow outside, just right.

I am not going so far as to say that New York that night was O Little Town of Bethlehem, but it was at least something different from the kind of New York Christmas best exemplified by a famous Christmas card sent out by a New York garage that year to all its customers. "Merry Christmas from the boys at the garage," that card said. "Second Notice."

For all that, it was hardly going to be, for me, a Merry Christmas. I am no Scrooge, but I am a curmudgeon and the word *merry* is not in the vocabulary of any self-respecting curmudgeon you would care to meet—on Christmas or any other day. You would be better off with a New York cabdriver, or even a Yankee fan.

There were other reasons why that particular Christmas had little chance to be one of my favorites. The fact that it was after seven o'clock and that I was still at my desk spoke for itself. The anti-cruelty society which I had founded a few years before was suffering growing pains—frankly, it is still suffering them—but at that particular time, they were close to terminal. We were heavily involved in virtually every field of animal work, and although we were doing so on bare subsistence salaries—or on no salary at all for most of us—the society itself was barely subsisting. It had achieved some successes, but its major accomplishments were still in the future.

And so, to put it mildly, was coin of the realm. Even its name, The Fund for Animals, had turned out to be a disappointment. I had, in what I had thought of as a moment of high inspiration, chosen it because I was certain that it would, just by its mention, indicate we could use money. The name had, however, turned out not only not to do the job but to do just the opposite. Everybody thought that we already had the money.

Besides the Fund's exchequer being low that Christmas Eve, so was my own. My writing career, by which I had supported myself since before you were born, was far from booming. I was spending so much time getting the Fund off the ground that I was four years behind on a book deadline and so many months behind on two magazine articles that, having run out of all reasonable excuses, one of the things I had meant to do that day was to borrow a line from the late Dorothy Parker and tell the editor I had really tried to finish but someone had taken the pencil.

As for my personal life, that too left something to be desired. Recently divorced, I was living in a small apartment, and although I was hardly a hermit—I had a goodly choice of both office parties and even friends' parties to go to that evening—still, this was not going to be what Christmas is supposed to be. Christmas is, after all, not a business holiday or a friends' holiday, it is a family holiday. And my family, at that point, consisted of one beloved daughter who lived in Pittsburgh and had a perfectly good family of her own.

On top of it all, there was a final irony in the situation. Although I had had animals in my life for as far back as I could remember, and indeed had had them throughout my marriage—and although I was working on animal problems every day of my life—I had not a single creature to call my own. For an animal person, an animal-less home is no home at all. Furthermore, mine, I was sure, was fated to remain that way. I travelled on an average of more than two weeks a month, and was away from home almost as much as I was there. For me, an animal made even less sense than a wife. You do not, after all, have to walk a wife.

I had just turned from the pleasant task of watching the snow outside to the unpleasant one of surveying the bills when the doorbell rang. If there had been anyone else to answer it, I would have told them to say to whoever it was that we already gave at home. But there was no one, so I went myself.

The caller was a snow-covered woman whom I recognized as Ruth Dwork. I had known Miss Dwork for many years. A former schoolteacher, she is one of those people who, in every city, make the animal world go round. She is a rescuer and feeder of everything from dogs to pigeons and is a lifetime soldier in what I have called the Army of the Kind. She is, however, no private soldier in that army—she makes it too go round. In fact, I always called her Sergeant Dwork.

"Merry Christmas, Sergeant," I said. "What can I do you for?"

She was all business. "Where's Marian?" she asked. "I need her." Marian Probst, my longtime and longer-suffering assistant, is an experienced rescuer, and I knew Miss Dwork had, by the very look of her, a rescue in progress. "Marian's gone," I told her. "She left about five-thirty, saying something about some people having Christmas Eve off. I told her she was a clock-watcher, but it didn't do any good."

Sergeant Dwork was unamused. "Well, what about Lia?" she demanded. Lia Albo is national coordinator of the Fund for Animals and an extremely expert rescuer. She, however, had left before Marian on—what else?—another rescue.

Miss Dwork was obviously unhappy about being down to me. "Well," she said, looking me over critically but trying to make the best of a bad bargain, "I need someone with long arms. Get your coat."

As I walked up the street with Sergeant Dwork, through the snow and biting cold, she explained that she had been trying to rescue a particular stray cat for almost a month, but that she had had no success. She had, she said, tried everything. She had attempted to lure the cat into a HavaHart trap but, hungry as he was and successful as this method had been in countless other cases, it had not worked with this cat. He had simply refused to enter any enclosure that he could not see his way out of. Lately, she confessed, she had abandoned such subtleties for a more direct approach. And, although she had managed to get the cat to come close to the rail fence at the end of the alley, and even to take bite-sized chunks of cheese from her outstretched fingers, she had never been able to get him to come quite close enough so that she could catch him. When she tried, he would jump away, and then she had to start all over the each-time-ever-more-difficult task of trying again to win his trust.

However, the very night before, Sergeant Dwork informed me, she had come the closest she had ever come to capturing the cat. That time, she said, as he devoured the cheese, he had not jumped away but had stood just where he was—nearer than he had ever been but still maddeningly just out of reach. Good as this news was, the bad news was that Miss Dwork now felt that she was operating against a deadline. The cat had been staying in the basement of the apartment building, but the superintendent of the building had now received orders to get rid of it before Christmas or face the consequences. And now the other workers in the building, following their super's orders, had joined in the war against the cat. Miss Dwork herself had seen someone, on her very last visit, throw something at him and hit him.

When we arrived at our destination, there were two alleyways. "He's in one or the other," Sergeant Dwork whispered. "You take that one, I'll take this." She disappeared to my left and I stood there, hunched in my coat with the snow falling, peering into the shaft of darkness and having, frankly, very little confidence in the whole plan.

The alley was a knife cut between two tall buildings filled with dim, dilapidated garbage cans, mounds of snowed-upon refuse, and a forbidding grate. And then, as I strained my eyes to see where, amongst all this dismal debris, the cat might be hiding, one of the mounds of refuse suddenly moved. It stretched and shivered and turned to regard me. I had found the cat.

As I said, that first sight was hardly memorable. He looked less like a real cat than like the ghost of a cat. Indeed, etched as he was against the whiteness of the snow all around him, he was so thin that he would have looked completely ghostlike, had it not been for how pathetically dirty he was. He was so dirty, in fact, that it was impossible even to guess as to what color he might originally have been.

When cats, even stray cats, allow themselves to get like that, it is usually a sign that they have given up. This cat, however, had not. He had not even though, besides being dirty, he was wet and he was cold and he was hungry.

And, on top of everything else, you could tell by the kind of off-kilter way he was standing that his little body was severely hurt. There was something very wrong either with one of his back legs or perhaps with one of his hips. As for his mouth, that seemed strangely crooked, and he seemed to have a large cut across it.

But, as I said, he had not given up. Indeed, difficult as it must have been for him from that off-kilter position, he proceeded, while continuing to stare at me unwaveringly, to lift a front paw—and, snow or no snow, to lick it. Then the other front paw. And, when they had been attended to, the cat began the far more difficult feat of hoisting up, despite whatever it was that was amiss with his hips, first one back paw and then the other. Finally, after finishing, he did what seemed to me completely incredible—he performed an all-four-paw, ears-laid-back, straight-up leap. It looked to me as if he was, of all things in such a situation, practicing his pounce.

An odd image came to my mind—something, more years ago than I care to remember, that my first college tennis coach had drilled into our team about playing three-set matches. "In the third set," he used to say, "extra effort for ordinary results." We loathed the saying and we hated even more the fact that he made us, in that third set, just before receiving serve, jump vigorously up and down. He was convinced that this unwonted display would inform our opponents that we were fairly bursting with energy—whether that was indeed the fact or not. We did the jumping, of course, because we had to, but all of us were also convinced that we were the only players who ever had to do such a silly thing. Now when I see, without exception, every top tennis player in the world bouncing like cork into the third set, I feel like a pioneer and very much better about the whole thing.

And when I saw the cat doing his jumping, I felt better too—but this time, of course, about him. Maybe he was not as badly hurt as at first I had thought.

In a moment I noticed that Sergeant Dwork, moving quietly, had rejoined me. "Look at his mouth," she whispered. "I told you they have declared war on him!"

⊳—┤ ◆⟩—○—⟨◆ ├—◅

Ours was to be a war too—but one not against, but for, the cat. As Sergeant Dwork quietly imparted her battle plan, I had the uneasy feeling that she obviously regarded me as a raw recruit, and also that she was trying to keep my duties simple enough so that even a mere male could perform them. In any case, still whispering, she told me she would approach the fence with the cheese cubes, with which the cat was by now thoroughly familiar, in her outstretched hand, and that, during this period, I apparently should be crouching down behind her but nonetheless moving forward with her. Then, when she had gotten the cat to come as close as he would, she would step swiftly aside and I, having already thrust my arms above her through the vertical bars of the fence, was to drop to my knees and grab. The Sergeant was convinced that the cat was so hungry that, at that crucial moment, he would lose enough of his wariness to go for the bait—and the bite—which would seal his capture.

Slowly, with our eyes focused on our objective, we moved out and went over the top. And just as we did so, indeed as I was crouching into position behind Sergeant Dwork, I got for the first time a good look at the cat's eyes peering at us.

They were the first beautiful thing I ever noticed about him. They were a soft and lovely and radiant green.

As Sergeant Dwork went forward, she kept talking reassuringly to the cat, meanwhile pointedly removing the familiar cheese from her pocket and making sure he would be concentrating on it rather than the large something looming behind her. She did her job so well that we actually reached our battle station at almost the exact moment when the cat, still proceeding toward us, albeit increasingly warily, was close enough to take his first bite from the Sergeant's outstretched hand.

That first bite, however, offered us no chance of success. In one single incredibly quick but fluid motion, the cat grabbed the cheese, wolfed it down, and sprang back. Our second attempt resulted in exactly the same thing. Again the leap, the grab, the wolf, and the backward scoot. He was simply too adept at the game of eat and run.

By this time I was thoroughly convinced that nothing would come of the Sergeant's plan. But I was equally convinced that we had somehow to get that cat. I wanted to get over that fence and go for him.

The Sergeant, of course, would have none of such foolhardiness, and, irritated as this made me, I knew she was right. I could never have caught the cat that way. The Sergeant was, however, thinking of something else. Wordlessly she gave me the sign of how she was going to modify her tactics. This time she would offer the cat not one but two cubes of cheese—one in each of her two outstretched hands. But this time, she indicated, although she would push her right hand as far as it would go through the fence, she would keep her left hand well back. She obviously hoped that the cat would this time attempt both bites before the retreat. Once more we went over the top—literally in my case, because I already had my hands through the fence over the Sergeant. And this time, just as she had hoped, the cat not only took the first bite but also went for that second one. And, at just that moment, as he was midbite, Sergeant Dwork slid to one side and I dropped to my knees.

As my knees hit the ground, my face hit the grate. But I did not even feel it. For, in between my hands, my fingers underneath and my thumbs firmly on top, was cat. I had him.

Surprised and furious, he first hissed, then screamed, and finally, spinning right off the ground to midair, raked both my hands with claws. Again I felt nothing, because by then I was totally engrossed in a dual performance—not letting go of him and yet somehow managing to maneuver his skinny, desperately squirming body, still in my tight grasp, albeit for that split second in just one hand, through the narrow apertures of the rail fence. And now his thinness was all-important because, skin and bones as he was, I was able to pull him between the bars.

Still on my knees, I raised him up and tried to tuck him inside my coat. But in this maneuver I was either overconfident or under-alert, because somewhere between the raising and the tucking, still spitting fire, he got in one final rake of my face and neck. It was a good one.

As I struggled to my feet, Sergeant Dwork was clapping her hands in pleasure, but obviously felt the time had now come to rescue me. "Oh," she said. "Oh dear. Your face. Oh my." Standing there in the snow, she tried to mop me with her handkerchief. As she did so, I could feel the cat's little heart racing with fear as he struggled to get loose underneath my coat. But it was to no avail. I had him firmly corralled, and, once again, with both hands.

The Sergeant had now finished her mopping and become all Sergeant again. "I'll take him now," she said, advancing toward me. Involuntarily, I took a step backwards. "No, no, that's all right," I assured her. "I'll take him to my apartment." The Sergeant would have none of this. "Oh no," she exclaimed. "Why, my apartment is very close." "So is mine," I replied, moving the cat even farther into the depths of my coat. "Really, it's no trouble at all. And anyway, it'll just be for tonight. Tomorrow, we'll decide—er, what to do with him."

Sergeant Dwork looked at me doubtfully as I started to move away. "Well then," she said, "I'll call you first thing in the morning." She waved a mittened hand. "Merry Christmas," she said. I wished her the same, but I couldn't wave back.

Joe, the doorman at my apartment building, was unhappy about my looks. "Mr. Amory!" he exclaimed. "What happened to your face? Are you all right?" I told him that not only was I all right, he ought to have seen the other guy. As he took me to the elevator, he was obviously curious about both the apparent fact that I had no hands and also the suspicious bulge inside my coat. Like all good New York City doormen, Joe is the soul of discretion—at least from tenant to tenant—but he has a bump of curiosity which would rival Mt. Everest. He is also, however, a good animal man, and he had a good idea that whatever I had, it was something alive. Leaning his head toward my coat, he attempted to reach in. "Let me pet it," he said. "No," I told him firmly. "Mustn't touch." "What is it?" he asked. "Don't tell anyone," I said, "but it's a saber-toothed tiger. Undeclawed, too." "Wow," he said. And then, just before the elevator took off, he told me that Marian was already upstairs.

I had figured that Marian would be there. My brother and his wife were coming over for a drink before we all went out to a party, and Marian, knowing I would probably be late, had arrived to admit them and hold, so to speak, the fort.

I kicked at the apartment door. When Marian opened it, I blurted out the story of Sergeant Dwork and the rescue. She too wanted to know what had happened to my face and if I was all right. I tried the same joke I had tried on Joe. But Marian is a hard woman on old jokes. "The only 'other guy' I'm interested in," she said, "is in your coat." I bent down to release my prize, giving him a last hug to let him know that everything was now fine.

Neither Marian nor I saw anything. All we saw, before his paws ever hit the ground, was a dirty tan blur, which, crooked hips notwithstanding, literally flew around the apartment—seemingly a couple of feet off the ground and all the time looking frantically for an exit.

In the living room I had a modest Christmas tree. Granted, it was not a very big tree—he was not, at that time, a very big cat. Granted, too, that this tree had a respectable pile of gaily wrapped packages around the base and even an animal figure attached to the top. Granted even that it was festooned with lights which, at rhythmic intervals, flashed on and off. To any cat, however, a tree is a tree and this tree, crazed as he was, was no exception. With one bound he cleared the boxes, flashed up through the branches, the lights, and the light cord and managed, somewhere near the top, to disappear again. "Now that's a good cat," I heard myself stupidly saying. "You don't have to be frightened. Nothing bad is going to happen to you here."

Walking toward the tree, I reached for where I thought he would be next, but it was no use. With one bound, he vanished down the far side and, flashing by my flailing arms, tried to climb up the inside of the fireplace. Fortunately the flue was closed, thus effectively foiling his attempt at doing a Santa Claus in reverse.

When he reappeared, noticeably dirtier than before, I was waiting for him. "Good boy," I crooned, trying to sound my most reasonable. But it was no use. He was gone again, this time on a rapid rampage through the bedroom—one which was in fact so rapid that not only was it better heard than seen but also, during the worst of it, both Marian and I were terrified that he might try to go through the window. When he finally materialized again in the hall, even he looked somewhat discouraged. Maybe, I thought desperately, I could reason with him now. Slowly I backed into the living room to get a piece of cheese from the hors d'oeuvre tray. This, I was sure, would inform him that he was among friends and that no harm would befall him. Stepping back into the hall, I found Marian looking baffled. "He's gone," she said. "Gone," I said. "Gone where?" She shook her head and I suddenly realized that, for the first time in some time, there was no noise, there was no scurrying, there was no sound of any kind. There was, in fact, no cat.

We waited for a possible reappearance. When none was forthcoming, obviously we had no alternative but to start a systematic search. It is a comparatively small apartment and there are, or so Marian and I at first believed, relatively few hiding places. We were wrong. For one thing, there was a wall-long bookshelf in the living room, and this we could not overlook, for the cat was so thin and so fast that it was eminently feasible that he had found a way to clamber up and wedge himself behind a stack of books on almost any shelf. Book by book, we began opening holes.

But he was not there. Indeed, he was not anywhere. We turned out three closets. We moved the bed. We wrestled the sofa away from the wall. We looked under the tables. We canvassed the kitchen. And here, although it is such a small kitchen that it can barely accommodate two normal-sized adults at the same time, we opened every cupboard, shoved back the stove, peered into the microwave, and even poked about in the tiny space under the sink.

At that moment, the doorbell rang. Marian and I looked at each other—it had to be my brother and his wife, Mary. My brother is one of only three men who went into World War II as a private and came out as a colonel in command of a combat division. He was, as a matter of fact, in the Amphibious Engineers, and made some fourteen opposed landings against the Japanese. He had also since served as deputy director of the CIA. A man obviously used to crises, he took one look at the disarray of the apartment. In such a situation, my brother doesn't talk, he barks. "Burglars," he barked. "It looks like a thorough job."

I explained to him briefly what was going on—and that

the cat had now disappeared altogether. Not surprisingly, while Mary sat down, my brother immediately assumed command. He demanded to know where we had not looked. Only where he couldn't possibly go, I explained, trying to hold my ground. "I don't want theories," he barked. "Where *haven't* you looked?" Lamely, I named the very top shelves of the closet, the inside of the oven, and the dishwasher. "Right," he snapped, and advanced on first the closets, then the oven, and last the dishwasher. And, sure enough, at the bottom of the latter, actually curled around the machinery and wedged into the most impossible place to get to in the entire apartment, was the cat. "Ha!" said my brother, attempting to bend down and reach him.

I grabbed him from behind. I was not going to have my brother trust his luck with one more opposed landing. Bravely, I took his place. I was, after all, more expendable.

Actually, the fact was that none of us could get him out. And he was so far down in the machinery, even he couldn't get himself out. "Do you use it?" my brother demanded. I shook my head. "Dismantle it," he barked once more. Obediently, I searched for screwdriver, pliers, and hammer and, although I am not much of a mantler, I consider myself second to no one, not even my brother, as a dismantler. My progress, however, dissatisfied my brother. He brushed me aside and went over the top himself. I made no protest—with the dishwasher the Amphibious Engineer was, after all, at least close to being in his element.

When my brother had finished the job, all of us, Mary included, peered down at the cat. And, for the first time since my first sight of him in the alley, he peered back. He was so exhausted that he made no attempt to move, although he was now free to do so. "I would like to make a motion," Marian said quietly. "I move that we leave him right where he is, put out some food and water and a litter pan for him—and leave him be. What he needs now is peace and quiet."

The motion carried. We left out three bowls—of water, of milk, and of food—turned out all the lights, including the Christmas lights, and left him.

That night, when I got home, I tiptoed into the apartment. The three bowls were just where we had left them—and every one of them was empty. There was, however, no cat. But this time I initiated no search. I simply refilled the dishes and went to bed. With the help of a sergeant, a colonel, and Marian, I now had, for better or for worse, for a few days at least, a Christmas cat.

Kitty at the Keyboard

STEVE DALE

Ricky, our talented Devon Rex cat, always liked to visit Boots Montgomery, the talented Tibetan terrier who lives across the hall. Boots knows the names of all seventy-five of her plush squeaky toys. No one on earth loves getting toys more than Boots; she can sniff out her toys and then proceeds to unwrap them.

The Christmas tree at the center of the living room is glorious, and veritably glows from the roaring fire in the fireplace on the other side of the room. It's two days before Christmas, we've been invited to share holiday cheer, drink, and gifts. Boots naturally finds and then unwraps her own gifts. Our dogs, Chaser and Lucy, appreciate the fact that they don't have thumbs; they don't even try opening their presents.

John, Boots's "dad," says, "Hey, look at that!" as Ricky, our then-five-year-old Devon Rex cat, does a Boots. Ricky finds his present, and then begins to rip apart the impeccably wrapped gift.

"Now what's going on?" asks John, as he begins to laugh. Ricky is halfway through the job, but then he falls over; gets up again, sniffs the gift, and then right back on the ground. Now, he's rubbing his cheeks against the present and meowing. "It looks like Ricky's been over-served," John says.

Of course, Ricky wasn't inebriated, but clearly he was telling us what was in the package: catnip.

The next day, on Christmas Eve, Ricky makes one of his many TV appearances. The local morning news shows are desperate for content on these slow news days. Ricky fills time with a musical interlude, playing tunes on his piano.

The news anchors at WMAQ-TV in Chicago aren't certain of exactly what it is that they're witnessing as Ricky casually pounds out his original jazz compositions.

On the air, anchor Art Norman says, "This isn't really a cat, is it?"

Art wasn't the first to wonder. After all, you don't see

a piano-playing kitty every day. And you don't see a Devon Rex every day, either. To some, Ricky doesn't even look like a member of the feline persuasion. He looks like a cute all-white Gremlin from the Steven Spielberg movie, with ears far too large for his elfin face. And like all Devon Rex cats, Ricky is folicly impaired. He has a single coat of soft curly hair (it feels like a chenille sweater), and a big spot in need of Rogaine on the top of his head.

Ricky was socialized from a young age, just hanging out on my shoulder like a parrot (he always had a leash and harness on in case he wanted to jump off, but I never needed to use it). Ricky would regularly go with the dogs to the pet store, to the local dry cleaner, to rent videos, or to the bank.

On one visit to the bank, a woman commented, "What a nice Chihuahua." After doing my transaction, and about to depart the building, a bank security guard stopped me. I thought, "I'm busted; they'll never allow me to take Ricky here again."

"Are batteries included with that thing?" he questioned.

Before I could answer, Ricky meowed. "Oh, that's cute—must be from a new Spielberg movie," he said.

The reason I toted my cat to these places is that I sought to demonstrate that cats can be socialized, too, and they can learn. So, I taught my little maestro to use his paws to play a plastic kid's piano. But Ricky's talents weren't limited to the musical arts; he was quite an athlete. Like a super feline hero, he could leap in a single bound over a prone dog in a "down/stay." He could also jump through a Hula Hoop.

TV crews loved Ricky. And he loved them. He actually learned on his own to look for the little red lights on cameras, and to follow them. Ricky worked for treats, but like most natural-born performers, he really craved attention.

I've never added up all of Ricky's TV appearances, but his piano playing has been shown on *National Geographic Explorer*, and *Pets: Part of the Family*, various Animal Planet programs as well as nearly all of Chicago's local news outlets.

When *Pet Project*, a Canadian TV show, heard about our four-legged musician, they sent a TV crew to our home. They even hired a piano teacher—a real piano teacher—to further Ricky's career. This was Chicago piano instructor Diane Aitken's second television appearance. Her first shot was on *The Oprah Winfrey Show*, conducting the studio audience and singer Luther Vandross in a sing-along of favorite Christmas songs.

She said that this was her first encounter with a student who purrs. In fact, at one point Ricky spontaneously began to meow as he played. Diane took it all so seriously. She stopped the taping. She picked Ricky up and looked into his eyes, admonishing, "You're no Luther Vandross—just play the song; we don't need to hear you." Amazing thing is, he listened.

Sounding very much like a piano teacher, she departed imploring with a straight face, "Practice, practice, practice, and one day you really will learn to play 'Three Blind Mice.'"

Ricky was a versatile pro. He could perform at pet stores, despite the fact that his piano and stage on a card table was more than once located across from gerbils. He could also perform outdoors. At the time, I figured if Garth Brooks can perform in Central Park, Ricky can play on the front steps of our condominium.

That's what Ricky was doing one day when a ten- or eleven-year-old boy with Down's syndrome walked by. He was enthralled with Ricky, staring expressionless and motionless for nearly five minutes. Suddenly, he began to laugh. We're not talking little giggles here; I mean big full-blown belly laughing.

His mother quietly told me, "Billy's father passed on two weeks ago. Everyone has tried to get him to talk, to react."

Just then, Billy, who was still in stitches, reached over to pet Ricky.

Ricky rubbed his face on Billy's arm, and nonchalantly walked up on his shoulder. Then Billy sat down and snuggled with Ricky, now in his lap. I don't know what secrets Billy shared, but he talked to Ricky for several minutes straight, sometimes laughing and sometimes crying. Just before he and his mom walked off, he looked at Ricky and said, "I love you," and then he kissed him. It's a kiss that I'll never forget.

That year, I remember Christmas was especially warm, at least by Chicago standards. It was about 32 degrees, and snow was falling lightly. Had I taken out his piano, it would have been the perfect backdrop for a chorus of "White Christmas." Instead we just slipped on his burnt orange sweater for a quick visit outside to play catch with the white beetles falling from the sky. That would be Ricky's last holiday.

The following summer, I lost my best buddy. He

succumbed at a young age, as musical geniuses sometimes seem to do. He died of an all-too-common heart disease in cats called feline hypertrophic cardiomyopathy (HCM).

As often happens with cats who have feline HCM, Ricky just dropped. One moment he was eating, the next moment he was dead. It's horrifying to see your beloved pet die. His tiny heart just gave out. Because of Ricky's HCM, the lower portion of his heart muscle was thicker than it should have been. Because of the thickening, his heart could not relax well or fill up with blood as it should have. If feline HCM is detected early, as it was with Ricky, a cat has a chance of at least a few more years of life, prolonged by medication.

When Ricky died, I felt as though I lost my best friend. I'm not sure I'll have another cat who knows what I'm thinking before I do it, or vice versa. Ricky and I had an astonishing psychic kind of connection. We were sort of the Lassie and Timmy of the cat world, except Ricky never rescued me from a well.

Every now and again I catch a rerun of Ricky on TV. I'm glad Ricky is still putting smiles on faces. But I don't need a TV rerun to remember Ricky. To some it might sound crazy, but a day doesn't go by that I don't think about Ricky, most especially whenever we have a white Christmas.

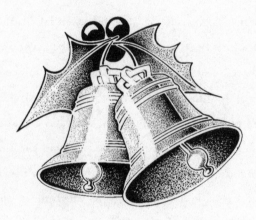

Spooky Gives Us a Scare

JANINE ADAMS

My cat, Joe, doesn't leave the house. But in the '60s and '70s when I was a child, no one (in my neighborhood at least) would dream of cooping their cat up indoors. So our gray domestic shorthairs, Spooky and Samantha, roamed the neighborhood. They could come inside whenever they wanted, though they didn't have a litter box and were asked to spend the night outside, except when the weather was bitterly cold.

Every morning, when my mother would bring in the morning paper, Samantha was on the porch waiting to come in. Spooky would come running out of nowhere to join her. But one early December Saturday morning when I was ten, only Samantha was on the porch when my mom opened the door. Spooky did not respond to her calls. He was nowhere in sight.

We shrugged it off, figuring that he'd found something especially fun to occupy him the night before. Every hour or so, one of us—either my parents, one of my brothers, or me, especially me—would open the front door, then the back door, and call out for him. No big gray cat with big green eyes would appear. By suppertime, we were worried. "If he's not back by morning, we'll send out a search team," my mom said. "But I think he'll be here in the morning."

I got up early the next morning, just as it was turning light. While the rest of the family slept, I crept downstairs and opened the door, holding my breath in anticipation. There was Samantha, who pushed her way in and noisily demanded an early breakfast. But no Spooky. I raced upstairs to tell my parents.

Despite the early hour, my parents didn't brush me off. They roused themselves, put on their robes, and came downstairs to talk with me about how we would find our kitty. As my mother put on coffee, my dad fed Samantha. I suggested we call the police, but my parents said they probably had more important things to work on than a missing cat. Once my brothers got up we sat at the breakfast table and made a list of all the things we would do to find Spooky. My oldest brother, Scott, who had an artistic flair, made a "lost cat" sign. We pasted a photo to the sign and photocopied it at my dad's office. Since Spooky was dark gray, the copied photo certainly didn't capture his beauty—or show off any distinguishing features—but we figured it was better than nothing.

My brothers and I pooled our money and were able to offer a $25 reward, which my parents doubled to $50. My father got in the car and drove around looking for Spooky. Scott, Larry, and I got on our bikes and plastered the immediate neighborhood with our signs. My mother stayed home in case Spooky appeared or someone called about him.

I was sure that our signs would do the trick. We were offering $50 for his return! But nightfall came on Sunday and there was no Spooky. Not even a telephone call about him.

I didn't want to go to school on Monday. "Let me stay home and look for Spooky," I begged my mom. She told me I could ride around on my bike looking for him after school until dark. "I'll put a 'lost cat' ad in the paper today," she reassured me. "That'll help us get him home."

After school, I pedaled everywhere I could think of. I stopped mail carriers, delivery truck drivers, anyone I could see. I gave them a flier and described Spooky. No one had seen him, but everyone said they'd keep an eye out for him. "Just call us if you see him," I said anxiously. "Our phone number's right on the piece of paper."

As the days crept by with no Spooky sightings, my hope began to fade. I couldn't imagine that my cat would run away. Maybe somebody stole him, I thought. Or maybe he got hit by a car. He was wearing only a bell on his collar—no tag—so if someone found his body they wouldn't know to call us. I started making deals with God. "Bring Spooky home and I'll do my homework every night before dinner," I bargained. Even though Spooky hadn't made it home, I began doing my homework as soon as I came home from looking for him, just in case it would help.

After our cat had been gone a week, I started to get desperate. Even though the police station in our small city was farther away than I was allowed to go on my bike, I grabbed one of the lost cat signs and took it to the police station.

I was barely tall enough to reach the top of the high counter. "Excuse me," I said politely. "My cat is lost." I noticed a look of amusement cross the desk sergeant's face, but then he looked down at me with a serious expression.

"How long has he been gone?" he inquired gravely.

"A whole week!" I wailed. "Here's his picture." I handed the cop our flier.

"Well, we haven't received any reports of a cat matching this description," he said to me kindly. "But I'll post this sign here on the bulletin board and ask the officers to keep an eye out for him. What's your cat's name?"

"It's Spooky. When he was a kitten, his eyes were so big it looked like he'd seen a ghost, so that's why we named him Spooky."

"He's a fine-looking cat," the sergeant said. "I hope we find him."

I pedaled home with new hope in my heart. If the whole police force of Walla Walla, Washington, was looking for Spooky, surely they'd find him. If he was still alive. I pushed that last thought out of my head and concentrated on the possibility that he would be found.

Meanwhile, poor Samantha seemed to be missing her brother. She wasn't eating as enthusiastically as she usually did. And she was more affectionate with us, particularly in the evening hours. She didn't complain as much. "She misses her brother," I observed to my parents.

"We all miss him," my father replied. I tried not to cry.

I took comfort in the fact that we were having relatively

warm weather for December. Every morning when I asked, my mother would check the paper and tell me how cold it had been the day before; it rarely dipped below freezing. "Maybe someone took him in thinking he was a stray," my mother said. I knew that idea was supposed to comfort me, but instead it made me mad. "He's my cat! They can't just keep him," I protested. But I realized it was better than some things that could have happened to him.

By the end of the second week of Spooky's absence, I started to lose faith. I still biked around the neighborhood after school looking for him and replacing any signs that had been taken down. But I came home after only an hour. I started to consider the fact that we'd never find Spooky. Sometimes I even thought about getting a new kitten.

I couldn't even get excited about Christmas, my favorite holiday. I was missing Spooky too much. On Christmas Eve, we decorated our tree and hung up our stockings. We hung Samantha's on the hearth right next to mine. Spooky's lay in the box.

"I guess we shouldn't hang up Spooky's stocking," I said to my mother.

"I don't see why not," she replied. "If Spooky comes home in time for Christmas, he'd be very sad not to find his stocking. And if he doesn't come home, Samantha can have his stocking stuffers."

I knew my mom was trying to make me feel better. But that day I'd officially given up hope. Spooky had been gone sixteen days. If he hadn't come home by now, I couldn't imagine we'd ever see him again.

On most Christmas Eves, I went to bed with thoughts of Christmas morning prancing around my mind, eager to go to sleep so I could wake up early and open presents. But this year, my heart was heavy and even the thought of opening presents couldn't cheer me up.

When Christmas morning arrived, for the first time in my life I didn't wake up at the crack of dawn. I didn't rush downstairs to see what Santa had brought. Instead, in my blue mood, I woke up later than usual and stayed in bed. "If I can't have Spooky, I don't want anything," I told myself, saying it out loud to emphasize the point. I just felt like wallowing in my misery.

At about 9:00, my mother tapped on my door. "Janine, are you okay?" she called. She opened the door a crack and stuck her head in. "I have something that I think will cheer you up."

"I don't want any Christmas presents," I told her morosely.

"I think you'll want this." She opened the door wide and to my amazement, a dirty gray cat was in her arms. She put him down gently on my bed and he came right up and nuzzled my face.

"Spooky, you're home!" I hollered, hugging him around the neck, my tears flowing into his fur. I let him go and took a look at him. His once sleek coat was dirty, with some tufts of hair missing. He was very thin. Some of his pads were raw, and closer inspection revealed that several of his claws were missing. One of his ears had a chink taken out of it. But he was alive. And he was in my arms.

"I opened the door this morning for the paper, and there he was," my mom told me. "He and Samantha walked in just like every morning." She told me that she had fed him—and that he was ravenous—before bringing him upstairs.

As we opened presents that morning—who could ask for a better Christmas present than Spooky's return?—we discussed what might have happened to our cat. Each of us had a theory (Larry thought he'd been abducted by aliens), but the one that seemed to make sense was that he'd somehow jumped into someone's car and been driven a distance away. Maybe he was trying to get away from something. Or maybe he found a car that smelled particularly interesting—he was always the inquisitive type. Perhaps someone picked him up thinking he was a stray and drove him to a distant home.

However it happened, we liked to think that when he finally had a chance to get away, he just started heading home. And that it took him all those days to get there. Who knew what adventures he'd been on in those two weeks. All we knew is that we were glad to have him home.

Spooky slept on my bed for about twenty-four hours, his belly full and his body and soul clearly exhausted. Samantha slept with him, though she took a nap break to have dinner. That night, my father didn't ask Spooky to sleep outside. He slept right in bed with me, capping my very best Christmas ever.

I'd like to say that we learned a lesson and never let Spooky and Samantha go outside again. But the truth is that they were let out at will. Thankfully, they were both on the porch each and every morning until the end of their lives. But whenever I start feeling sorry that my twenty-first-century cat, Joe, can't go outside, I think about Spooky and what he must have gone through during the seventeen days he was gone. Then I hug Joe and make sure he's happy inside.

My Mother's Cat

Renie Burghardt

My family lived in Hungary during World War II. When my nineteen-year-old mother died two weeks after giving birth to me, I inherited her cat, Paprika. He was a gentle giant with deep-orange stripes and yellow eyes that gazed at me tolerantly as I dragged him around wherever I went. Paprika was ten years old when I came into this world. He had been held and loved by my mother for all ten years of his life, while I had never known her, so I considered him my link to her. Each time I hugged Paprika tightly to my chest, I warmed to the knowledge that my mother had held him, too.

"Did you love her a lot?" I often asked Paprika as we snuggled on my bed.

"Meow!" he would answer, rubbing my chin with his pink nose.

"Do you miss her?"

"Meow!" Paprika's large yellow eyes gazed at me with a sad expression.

"I miss her, too, even though I didn't know her. But Grandma says Mother is in heaven and watching over us from there. Since you and I are both her orphans, I know it makes her happy that we have each other." I would always say these words to Paprika, for they were most comforting thoughts to me.

"Meow!" Paprika would respond, climbing on my chest and purring.

"And it makes me so very happy that we have each other," I would tell Paprika.

I'd hold him close, tears welling up in my eyes. Paprika would reach up with his orange paw and touch my face gently. I was convinced that this cat understood me, and I knew that I understood him. His love and devotion were always obvious.

My maternal grandparents raised me because the war had taken my young father away, too. He served in the army and visited me occasionally, but I could not live with him. As I grew older, the fighting intensified. Soon we were forced to become migrants in search of safer surroundings.

In the spring of 1944, when I was eight years old, Paprika and I snuggled in the back of a wooden wagon as we traveled around Hungary. During the numerous air raids of those terrible times, we had to scramble to find safety in a cellar, a closet, or a ditch. Paprika always stayed in my arms, for I refused to go anywhere without him. How could I ever be separated from him? After all, one of the first stories my grandparents ever told me was that my dying mother had begged them to take care of her cat as well as her baby.

After Christmas of 1944, when we were almost killed in a bombing, Grandfather decided that we would be safer in a rural area. We soon settled into a small house that had a cemetery as its neighbor. Grandfather and some helpful neighbors built a bunker for us nearby.

On an early spring day in 1945, we spent the entire night in that bunker. Paprika was with me, of course, because I refused to leave without my cat. Warplanes buzzed, tanks rumbled, and bombs whistled and exploded over our heads all night. I clung to Paprika, my grandmother held on to both of us, and we prayed the entire time. Paprika never panicked in that bunker. He just stayed in my arms, comforting me with his presence.

Finally everything grew deathly still, and Grandfather decided that it would be safe for us to return to the house. Cautiously, we crept into the light of early dawn and headed across the field. The brush crackled under our feet as we walked. I shivered, holding Paprika tightly. Suddenly there was a rustle in the bushes ahead. Two men jumped out and pointed machine guns at us.

"Stoi!" one of the men shouted. We knew the word meant "Stop!"

"Russians!" Grandfather whispered. "Stand very still and keep quiet."

But Paprika, who had never left me through all the traveling and the bombings, suddenly leapt out of my arms. So instead of obeying Grandfather, I darted between the soldiers and scooped up the cat. The tall, dark-haired young soldier approached me. I cringed, holding Paprika against my chest. To my astonishment, the soldier reached out and gently petted my cat.

"I have a little girl who is about your age," he said. "She's back in Russia. She has a cat just like this one." As he smiled at us, I looked up into a pair of kind brown eyes, and my fear vanished. My grandparents sighed with relief.

Later that morning, we found out that the Soviet occupation of our country was in progress. Many atrocities occurred in Hungary in the following months, but because the young soldier had taken a liking to me and my cat, our lives were spared. He visited us often and brought treats for Paprika and me. Then one day, a few months later, he had some news. "I've been transferred to another area, Malka ['little one'], so I won't be able to visit you anymore," he said. "But I have a gift for you." He reached into his pocket and pulled out a necklace. It was beautiful, and it had a turquoise Russian Orthodox cross on it. He placed it around my neck. "You wear this at all times, Malka. God will protect you from harm. And you take good care of your kitten."

I hugged the soldier tightly, then watched with tears in my eyes as he left.

Throughout the trying times that persisted in our country, Paprika's love made things easier for me to bear. He was my comfort and my best friend, and he rarely left my side.

In the fall of 1945, Grandfather went into hiding. He had spoken up about the atrocities taking place in our country, and he didn't want to be imprisoned as a dissident by the new Communist government. Grandmother and I expected Christmas to be solemn, but it then turned into my worst nightmare. I awoke on Christmas morning to find Paprika lifeless and cold, still curled up next to me. I picked up his body, held him close, and sobbed uncontrollably. He was nineteen years old, and I was only nine.

"I will always love you, Paprika. I will never give my heart to another cat," I vowed through my tears. "Never, ever!"

"Paprika's spirit is in heaven now with your mama, sweetheart," my grandmother said, trying to comfort me. But my heart was broken on that terrible Christmas Day.

Grandfather remained in hiding until the fall of 1947. At that time, we were finally able to escape Communist Hungary by hiding among some ethnic Germans who were being deported to Austria. When we got to Austria, we lived in a displaced-persons camp for four years. But there was hope for us: We were accepted for immigration to the United States of America. In September of 1951, we boarded an old Navy ship and were on our way to America.

Christmas of 1951 was our first in this wonderful new

country. The horrors of war and the four years of hardship in a refugee camp were behind us. A new life, filled with hope, lay ahead.

On that Christmas morning, I awoke to a tantalizing aroma wafting through the house: Grandmother was cooking her first American turkey. Grandfather, meanwhile, pointed to one of the presents under the Christmas tree. The package seemed to be alive, for it was hopping around to the tune of "Jingle Bells" that was playing on the radio. I rushed over, pulled off the orange bow, and lifted the lid from the box.

"Meow," cried the present, jumping straight into my lap and purring. It was a tiny orange tabby kitten. When I looked into his yellow eyes, the vow I'd made in 1945 to never love another cat crumbled away, and love filled my heart again.

I do believe my mother smiled down approvingly at us from heaven that Christmas Day, while Paprika's spirit purred joyfully at her side. Since then, there have been many other cats in my life, but the memory of my mother's cat will live in my heart forever.

The Real Thing

BETH ADELMAN

There's an old legend that at midnight on Christmas Eve, all the animals in the world speak in human voices—a gift from God originally bestowed upon the animals in the manger in Bethlehem.

The legend originated in Eastern Europe, but it has echoes in many other stories from many cultures around the world. We humans long to understand the animals around us, and the closer we live with them, the deeper our longing. Our cats are members of our family, but as well as we come to know them, they are also always a little mysterious—part of us and yet apart. Sometimes we look at their exquisite faces and can't help wonder what they are thinking.

Wouldn't it be wonderful if they could tell us? I remember the thrill I experienced when I took a trip to Spain and was finally able to use my high school Spanish to understand and be understood in another language. I felt as if I had opened up a new world. How much more thrilling—and more elusive—it is to communicate with another species.

In fact, we humans have been trying to do just that for decades, teaching apes to use sign language and parrots to talk. And even sneaking into the barn on Christmas Eve, hoping for a miracle. In all these efforts, we expect the animals to speak our language. As unreasonable as this is (after all, we're supposed to be the smarter ones), the animals do their best to accommodate us. Their limits seem not to be in their ability and desire to use our language, but in their physical makeup. Apes have the manual dexterity required to sign and birds have the syrinx that enables them to make a variety of complex sounds. But most animals lack the hands and the voice needed to communicate the way we do.

So where does that leave our cats? Actually, it leaves them with an astonishing array of body postures, facial expressions, sounds (cats can make more than one hundred distinctive vocal sounds, while dogs make about ten), and even ways of manipulating their fur and whiskers, all of which they use to tell the world exactly what's on their minds. And that's not counting the scent and visual markers they leave behind for later reading. So while we're waiting for a Christmas miracle, maybe all we really need is a feline-English dictionary.

Our cats, of course, have never needed a dictionary. They've already got the interspecies communication thing figured out. They are masters at reading our little gestures, body postures, and facial expressions. They know just from looking at us when we are mad, scared, sick, happy, ready to go to bed, or ready to play with them. They notice the little things we do that we're not even aware of. We may be able to hide things from our mothers, but we can't hide anything from our cats.

When it comes to communicating with us, they try hard to speak to us the way we prefer. The same study that counted how many types of vocalizations cats are capable of also found that they vocalize a lot more to us than they do to other cats. In other words, cats noticed all on their own that while *they* communicate mainly with scents and body postures, *we* communicate mainly with sounds. So they speak to us with more sounds and fewer postures, hoping we'll get the idea.

Then why don't we? Why does communicating with them seem so elusive? Why do we think we need a miracle?

I think it's because we humans rely so heavily on communicating with words that when the words aren't there, we don't really trust ourselves to understand. We live so closely with our cats that we usually know what they want and we often know what they're thinking. We understand them, but we don't believe we do.

There are times when my cats look very earnestly into my eyes, their faces clearly marked with emotion. Sometimes they squeak or yip or meow. Sometimes they use their body posture to lead me somewhere (usually a place where they can settle down next to me). Sometimes they simply tremble with delight that I am looking at them and softly saying their names. At all these times, they are communicating with me with supreme sincerity, and I try to be equally sincere in my attempts to understand them. Often that means just quieting my mind and watching them carefully. When I do, I have flashes of understanding that might be insight or might be something more—I am not willing to rule out anything, because animals communicate in all kinds of ways we don't completely understand. The communication is real, and we have to trust the ways we experience it.

We are wise, I think, to be wary of interpreting our cats' messages as if they came from a human. "She thinks she's a person" is a cute thing to say about a cat, but it's also an easy way to lose the very special wonder of establishing a connection with another, decidedly nonhuman, species. Reaching out to our cats takes us outside ourselves in a way that opens up our minds and our hearts. But in our wisdom and our wariness about thinking of our cats as human, we sometimes ignore our intuition and limit the ways we are willing to understand the creatures in our midst. We don't trust what we know in our hearts to be true. So, for example, we want to believe our cats love us, but somehow, despite all the evidence of our lives with them, we're not sure if it's really true. If only they could say the words!

Until very recently, it was "accepted wisdom" among scientists that animals don't feel any emotions at all—not even love. Scientists came to this conclusion because the animals they studied had never described or shown their emotions in a way that the scientists could quantify in an experiment. But just because you can't study something scientifically doesn't mean it's not real.

One strange and sad result of this "accepted wisdom" was a conversation I had with a friend who is a school science teacher. She told me, "Whenever I sit down on the couch, my cat always sits right next to me and presses her head into my hands until I pet her. I know it's really all about food and my cat doesn't actually love me. But it's still so nice when she snuggles up with me, and I just tell myself it seems like love."

I said, "If it *seems like* love, why do you think it isn't?" But what I was really thinking was, How could any person live with a cat and think she doesn't feel fear, humor, excitement, grief, pleasure, and, most of all, love? There's no question that mealtimes are among the highlights of any cat's day, but so are play times, snuggle times, and purr times. How could every single friendly interaction we have with our cats be a bribe for food? Nobody wants to believe that. And so we wish that on Christmas Eve the animals would tell us, "You were right all along. Our love is the real thing."

In fact, they *do* tell us, if only we would trust our hearts. I know their love is real, and so do you.

How do I know? You might as well ask me how I know my husband loves me. I know because of the way he treats me, the way he looks at me, the way he seeks out my company and never seems to get bored with me, even after all these years. I know because things are more fun for both of us when he's around, because dire problems don't seem so dire when we're together, because he takes extra good care of me when I'm sick or just feeling low, because he puts me at the center of his life. He doesn't say "I love you" every day, but every day I know he does.

In their own way, my cats also do all of these things. They follow me from room to room—even pushing their way into the bathroom to be with me. They're not always right next to me, but they're usually nearby. When I sit down on the couch, they sometimes wrestle to decide who gets to sit next to me. If I'm in another room and they call to me, they keep calling until I answer. When I'm sick, they spend more time napping with me. When I'm sad, they snuggle up extra close. They would always rather play with me than with each other, and they make up games and then teach me the rules. They bring me their little mousey prey toys as gifts, dropping them at my feet and looking up at me with devotion. They run to my side when I call them—just for the reward of a hug. They purr when I look into their eyes and say their names. I know they love me because they *act like* they love me. That's how every creature on earth, human or animals, shows their love. It's how my cats know I love them.

You don't have to wait for Christmas. The miracle is already here, snuggled up next to you. Sometimes it's hard for us to trust the experience of our own lives and hearts. But when we observe our cats closely, with an open mind and an open heart, we see the richness of their emotional and their spiritual lives. We see it in the way they act. We see it in their faces. We see it in their eyes. When you do, trust what you see and feel. You know it's the real thing.

Bengal Turkey Divine

Miriam Fields-Babineau

s I sat down to Christmas Eve dinner, prepared by my gourmet chef husband, the phone rang. Not the normal ting-a-ling I would receive when being called by a client, but the *Dragnet* intro that signaled a call from my mother.

How nice, I thought. *Mother is calling to wish us a Happy Holiday.*

No way. Mother didn't celebrate Christmas, nor did she like my husband. She was most probably calling for another reason. She was seventy-three and well into senile dementia, making her difficult to take at times, along with being very accident prone. I knew I had to answer the phone. I pulled out the chair, giving my husband a resigned look, which he returned. I walked to the kitchen phone, followed by my two Bengal cats. Chewy and Sorceress had also been waiting for their holiday meal. (My husband always sneaked a few tidbits to them from the table.) The feast would have to wait.

"Hello," I said, picking up the phone, acting as though I had no idea who the caller was.

"Margo!" exclaimed Mother. "Margo. Help!"

I stiffened. Something *had* happened after all. Then again, she often did this just to get me to visit her. Her life, and thereby mine whenever I communicated with her, was total chaos.

"Yes, Mother," I answered. "What's up?"

Mother sighed, then whimpered.

Sometimes she could put on a real act. She knew how to get to me.

"Are you okay?" I asked. "Are you sick?"

"Oh no, Margo. He's gone. I don't know where he went." I tilted my head thinking, he, who?

"Mother?"

"Beamer, Margo," she scoffed, now upset with me for being unable to read her mind. "Beamer's gone. He must've run through the door as I was putting the trash out and I didn't see it. I've looked all over the house and

I can't find him. Oh, Margo. I can't see out there and he's gone. Just gone!"

Beamer was Mother's Himalayan cat. I had arranged for her to take in a rescued cat from the breeder who had given me my Bengals. After her dog died last year she really needed company and, since she wasn't getting around very well, cats would be easier to care for while offering companionship. Hence came Beamer. Beamer was two years old and very shy. There was no way someone could walk right up to him. The only person he ever wanted to spend time with was Mother, sitting on her lap while she wrote on her computer.

"I'm so sorry, Mother. You think he might turn up in a bit? He's never been out before and is probably frightened. He might be at the door this very minute."

"Margo," her voice lowered. I could picture the look on her face—jaw set, eyes narrowed, mouth tight. "I'm looking out the door *this very minute* and he's not there. You need to come here and help me find him. He's going to disappear just like the other cats around here."

"What other cats?"

"Nancy Hanover's Persian, Fooey. And, Missy Hendridge's cat, Cocoa. Her daughter is still in tears over it. Then, there's Sibyl's cat, Moonie. Why, she's been gone over a month. I've never seen Sibyl so depressed. I've heard rumors from other neighbors about how it's like an epidemic. Even cats that are always indoors are disappearing. They haven't been found dead in the road, or picked up by animal control. Just vanished."

Mother was panicking and would surely collapse if she kept it up. Though her health hadn't been the best lately, she still continued to work and remain involved in many activities. Mother was never someone who would slow herself down. Worse yet, her eyesight was really bad. She could hardly recognize a person directly in front of her, much less a cat. At night she was totally blind. There was no way she could go outside and search for Beamer.

"Mother, he's not going to come to me."

"He might."

I looked across the room at my husband carving the golden brown turkey, the table laden with candied yams, venison stuffing, garlic mashed potatoes, creamy gravy, and freshly baked biscuits. The smell wafted through the house. My stomach rumbled, saliva collecting in my mouth. I had starved myself the entire day so that I could eat this meal. My Bengals, being part Asian wild-cat with high prey drives and never-ending appetites, rubbed against my legs, Chewy meowing loud enough to make the ear not attached to the phone ache. He'd been looking forward to the meal as well. Spoiled rotten cat.

"Mother. It's Christmas Eve. Dinner's ready right now. I was just about to eat."

"Sure. You eat while my cat gets killed."

There was the guilt trip that always got to me. My entire body sagged. I did care if the cat were to be killed. I adored cats; I trained them for a living.

My husband would be really upset. He'd been cooking as long as I'd been starving myself. He and Mother had never gotten along, unless he was doing something Mother needed done. Though we had been together for over twenty years, Mother still hated him to the molecular level. Not that he didn't try; Mother was just very stubborn. The looks she gave him were enough to freeze up a hot tub filled with roiling water.

"Okay, Mother. Give me a few minutes. Who knows what kind of traffic I'm going to run into on Christmas Eve; everyone doing their last-minute shopping and such."

"Great. See you soon, Margo." Her voice brightened. She'd won . . . again.

My husband knew as I walked into the dining room. His shoulders slumped. "You have to go, huh. After all this work I put into dinner." He rubbed his face, ruminating, staring at the turkey he'd just carved into juicy slices. "What's the problem this time?"

As I explained the situation to him, his lips thinned with anger. "It's just another celebration she's going to destroy. I swear she does this intentionally." He sighed. "But, you've gotta go. I know."

Chewy sat at his feet and meowed up at him. Sorceress joined in, walking around Chewy, her tail in the air, flicking from side to side. She often copied whatever he did, especially when it came to her belly.

"Sorry, guys. Not now," he said to the hungry cats. "We've all gotta wait until Marcella Finney gets her cat back."

He looked up at me. "You need me to come with you?"

I knew he really didn't want to. I also knew my mother wouldn't want him to.

"No, Hon. You don't have to."

He visibly relaxed.

"Well, why don't you take the cats. You'll never be able to catch Beamer without Chewy and Sorceress to help track him down."

Once, when my mother had stayed with us for a week while ill, her cat Beamer had met with Chewy. Chewy attacked Beamer causing him to leave a puddle on the carpet. Beamer had to be locked in my mother's room so that cat fur wouldn't be flying around the house for a week. The entire time they had stayed, Chewy was at the door, screaming at Beamer. That, paired with my mother's demands (all she needed was a bell and the situation would've been complete), made the week a living hell.

Yes, taking my cats might be a good idea. I put on their harnesses, slipped on my heavy winter coat, and loaded us all into the SUV.

Despite some traffic, I arrived less than an hour later.

My mother lived in northwest Washington, D.C., near Rock Creek Park, a place inhabited by the kind of people she felt were at her "level"—doctors, lawyers, and diplomats. Despite the fact that she survived on her sole income as a clinical psychologist, she had bought a home in this area and now had to work hard to afford to keep it. It would've been below her station to sell her house in northern Virginia and buy a condo, giving her less work to do in many ways. No. She had to have a brick house, among the professional elite.

I shook my head every time I thought of it. For such an intelligent woman she had no common sense. But she sure knew how to lay a guilt trip. After all, here I was on Christmas Eve, an empty belly, husband at home waiting, helping her find her cat.

I went into Mother's house and called out to her. As anxious as she was for my assistance, I had expected her to meet me at the door. No sign of her. No note, not that I could've found it anyway. Clutter is a congenial means of describing the inside of her home.

Oh no, I thought. *She went out looking for Beamer. Now I have to look for her.*

This presented a real problem, as I had brought a dominant cat to track another cat, not a search-and-rescue dog. I went to the back door and called out. No answer.

Remembering that the police would not do anything unless a person was missing for a prolonged period of time, I gave up the idea of calling them. It was up to me. I knew Mother was likely out searching for Beamer, so I decided to do the same, hoping to run into her.

Returning to my SUV, I gathered my cats. Chewy bristled with happiness at the chance to strut outdoors.

He pulled at his leash, raring to go. Quickly, I put on Sorceress's leash as well and allowed them to jump out of the vehicle. I was pulled down the block immediately as Chewy single-mindedly headed into the cold, damp darkness; Sorceress trotting alongside him. Whenever they're on a mission, whether searching for food or general mischief, they are joined at the hip, tails up, waving in the air, big eyes peeled on the ground before them, noses quivering with delight. The hunt was on.

The Bengals weren't bothered by the wet sidewalk, the occasional car splashing through puddles, or the bright decorations covering the neighborhood houses. They were on the prowl and nothing deterred them from their goal. I raced down the sidewalk behind them, pulled by double Bengal power, calling out Mother's name.

Chewy suddenly stopped, jaw dropping, nose quivering in the air, tail stiff. He turned his head toward a Tudor-style home, the eaves covered in twinkling lights.

"Is this it, Chewy?" I asked. "Is Beamer in here?"

Chewy looked up at me and grinned as only a cat can. Instead of seeing his big blue eyes, I saw the red reflection from his corneas giving him a devilish appearance. Sorceress rubbed against him, softly mewing, tail caressing his side. This had to be the house. Chewy's nose was always accurate, especially when it concerned food, or a cat he hated. One never knew which until the time came.

Mother had once told me who lived there. Bernard Talbot. He was *the doctor* in the neighborhood. Part of why the house prices were so high, according to Mother. I didn't counter that the housing prices probably had more to do with the location than anything else. When Mother gets an idea in her head, no matter how ridiculous, it's real to her. This includes past events, the reasons for current world crisis, and her unreasonable hatred of her children's spouses. Arguing never accomplished anything.

I followed the Bengals to Doctor Talbot's front door. The cats slowed, suddenly apprehensive. The front door was painted the color of dried blood. I stood in the shadowy portico and pushed the doorbell—feeling like a trick-or-treater on Halloween instead of someone searching for a cat on Christmas Eve. All Talbot would have to do is answer the door wearing a sheet, say "Boo!" and I'd probably have run, screaming, to my SUV, dragging my cats behind me.

The cats circled in front of the door, Sorceress stopping to sharpen her nails on the thick rubber doormat. Chewy pushed his nose against the door, rubbing, pushing, anxious to go inside.

I rang the bell again.

I was beginning to think no one was home when the front door opened a crack. A middle-aged man, with dark brown tousled hair and a three-day beard, peeked out.

"What do you want?" he asked, his voice low.

Mother had often told me about how great her neighborhood was and how everyone watched out for each other. It wasn't quite the greeting I'd expected.

"Hi, I'm Margo, Marcella Finney's daughter. She lives down your street?" Pointing for emphasis.

He showed no sign of recognition.

"Mother has lost her cat. A Himalayan named Beamer. I was wondering if you've seen him?"

"No, I . . ."

Chewy and Sorceress pushed into his house through the slot in the doorway, straining at the leash for me to follow.

"Hey, get those cats outta here," he bellowed. "I'm allergic. They can't be in here!"

Talbot's cheeks turned bright red with anger. He grabbed for Sorceress's leash, only to have Chewy bite his hand. No one messed with Chewy's girl.

"Ouch! Your freakin' cat bit me!"

As Talbot let go of the door to examine the damage to his left hand, it swung open revealing a plush interior, fully decorated for the holiday with candles, lighted tree, cards lining the fireplace mantel, and a full dinner upon the table, similar to the one I had almost been able to enjoy, only his turkey wasn't carved yet, and there was only one place setting. He lived alone. A chair was haphazardly pushed away from an otherwise neat table as though the occupant had arisen quickly.

Did he get a call from his mother, too?

I pulled back on the Bengals' leashes hoping to draw them out of Talbot's house. Chewy struggled and twisted, his long, sinewy body slipping free of the harness. He ran into the house toward the dining room.

"Oh my God," I said. "I'm so sorry. I'd better get him. Please excuse me for a moment."

I squirmed through the open doorway, unmindful of Talbot's reaction. My only thoughts were to retrieve my cat and continue the quest for Mother and Beamer.

Sorceress screeched for Chewy, her voice ranging from a throaty growl to a high-pitched shriek. Her nails dug into the Persian area rugs along our path and left rents in the polished wood floor between. Chewy continued, trotting briskly toward the dining room. I could only hope that his goal wasn't the dining table.

I'd have a lot to apologize for.

"What the hell're you doing?" Talbot yelled. "Get your stinking felines out of my house!"

The cats took me to a closed door beside the dining room. Chewy pushed his paws under the door and hissed, his tail puffed to the extreme. Sorceress crouched low, nose quivering as she sniffed, a low growl echoing from her throat.

I looked at the dark stained wood panel door, then back at Talbot, whom I had expected to follow me. He hadn't. In fact, he had reseated himself at the table, head in his hands.

Odd, I thought. *He looks morose. Why would that be?*

Yowling cats returned my attention to the door. Only, when I looked down, it wasn't my cats that were yowling. In fact, both remained crouched at the base of the door, growling and panting. The yowling was coming from the other side of the door.

Why would someone allergic to cats have them?

Again, I looked back at Talbot. He remained seated, not even looking at me.

I opened the door. Chewy and Sorceress rushed in.

As I crossed the threshold and moved into the room I could hardly believe my eyes. My heart thumped so hard I felt it would come up my throat and out my mouth.

Mother was seated on a high-back chair, arms tied at her sides with a long strip of cotton, a ball of material in her mouth, held in place with another strip of material. She squirmed from side to side, eyes bulging from their sockets. On two sides of the room were metal cages, stacked three high. There had to be at least fifteen cats in them. The room reeked from urine; I should've been able to smell this cattery from outside the door, yet I hadn't. (That might've been due to a good ventilation system.) Near Mother's chair was a small operating table of the sort used in veterinary practice surgical suites. The operating table was clean, but for a few stray black hairs, and rope restraints that lay in wait for the next feline victim.

I let go of the Bengals' leashes, and ran to Mother, immediately untying the gag on her mouth.

"Mother!" I wailed. "What the hell's going on?" I untied her arms.

"Margo," she answered, taking deep breaths. "Talbot, he . . ." She stopped in mid-sentence. Her eyes went wide as she stared at something over my shoulder and pointed, screaming, "Here he comes! Margo, WATCH OUT!"

I pivoted around, partially ducking as a reflex, only to miss impact with Talbot's Christmas turkey, the juices splattering my face and neck.

"Mom! Call the police!" I yelled, hoping Talbot would concentrate on braining me with the cooked bird and not go after Mother as well.

From the corner of my eye I saw Chewy with his paws on Beamer's cage. He licked his lips. Some of the roast turkey juices had hit him in his face. Sorceress sniffed the floor. They both turned away from the screaming cats in the cages, searching for the source of the delectable drippings, noses quivering, paws kneading the tile floor. Food first, screaming cats later.

Talbot raised the glazed, dripping hunk of bird for another strike.

Chewy and Sorceress looked up at the turkey, blue and green eyes locking on their goal. What's more, Talbot gave them "The Signal." (My cats had learned to climb fifty-foot ropes to reach a platform from which they would jump. Their signal: My hands held high in the air. They didn't need any more of an invitation.)

Chewy jumped onto Talbot's right thigh and dug in for the climb. Sorceress, not to be denied her just reward, jumped onto his other thigh. Together they worked their way up the doctor's body, claws leaving bloody runes in his flesh, his slacks shredded.

Bernard Talbot screamed with pain. He stood still, body quivering, turkey still held high, its purpose forgotten to all but the cats. Chewy and Sorceress didn't make any noise as they moved upward. I knew the Bengals would soon reach the turkey and by then Talbot would sink to the floor. Glancing behind me to make sure Mother was gone, I searched for a weapon. Nothing but a tray of surgical instruments. Not good. I'd be bludgeoned with a turkey far faster than I could cut the man's throat with a scalpel. As Chewy and Sorceress reached Talbot's shoulders, forepaws stretching up his arms, I ran from the operating room to the living room, where a fireplace, complete with merry flames of brilliant red, orange, and yellow, greeted me. A fireplace poker, its sharp end coated in gray ash, lay against the side.

Weapons. Far more useful than a turkey.

I had just gotten my hand around the fireplace poker when I heard heavy footsteps. Talbot had emerged from the back room, sans turkey, blood seeping through his torn clothing. I held the poker high, ready to swing.

"You stop right there, Mister. Or, I swear, I'll brain you!" I said in my bravest voice, the fireplace poker shaking as hard as my knees.

Mother peeked out from behind the kitchen door, eyes wide with fright, the lines in her face flat, cheeks red, and lips swollen where the gag had bruised her skin.

"I called 911," she said, bolstering my courage. "They'll be here soon, Bernard. You may as well give it up." She remained half hidden behind the kitchen door, ready to bolt if Talbot decided to go after her again.

"You'd best just give up," I echoed Mother. I was so frightened I couldn't think up my own reprisal.

The sound of sirens emerged as through a distant fog. I knew the cops would be at least another five minutes. Long enough to make a difference in my life, or death, or somewhere between.

A long wail came out of Chewy's mouth, joined by Sorceress's mewl as they both sauntered into the room, tails waving in the air, faces covered in turkey juice. The Bengals stepped high with pleasure, their bellies distended from their Christmas meal. As much as they wanted to they couldn't eat more than their stomach capacity.

Talbot's grimace of anger fell to desperation.

"Keep those ferocious beasts away from me!" he screamed, arms stretched out before him as though warding off evil spirits.

I had the upper hand.

"You'd better give up and sit down or I'll set 'em on you again," I warned.

As though I had anything to do with it the first time.

He sagged into a chair, chin dropped to his chest. He held his hand out to me, like a frightened dog showing active submission. If he licked his lips, the picture would be complete.

"Alright. Alright. I can't go on like this," he sobbed. "I'm trying to do something for other people and I get stomped on by my very subjects."

"What subjects?" I asked. "Cats?"

He glanced up at me and waved in dismissal. I lowered the fireplace poker a bit as it was getting heavy. Chewy and Sorceress rubbed against my legs and then began grooming each other, happily licking off the remnants of their feast.

"No. No," he sighed. "The cats were used to test the

drug. It wasn't for them. It's for women."

"Women?" Mother and I asked simultaneously. Mother had entered the room behind the Bengals, using them for cover. Talbot would have to go through them before he could get to her.

"I've discovered a new drug that helps with the female libido. I couldn't keep taking cats from the shelters or it would look suspicious, so I picked up the neighborhood cats."

"They're mostly fixed, wise guy," Mother said. "Besides, Beamer's a male. I thought you were a physician. You'd know these things."

Talbot lifted his head and looked at Mother. "Of course I knew, Mrs. Finney. But what if I could design a drug that worked on post-menopausal women? Fixed cats were the perfect subjects." He looked at the floor. "I didn't know if they were male or female until I brought them home and looked. Yours was an accident. I was going to let him go tomorrow."

"Why not do your experiments in a lab at the university?" I asked.

"It wasn't sanctioned by the department," Talbot answered. "I had this idea and it just couldn't wait for all the bureaucracy. There's already a drug entering the market, but it's got loads of side effects. Mine didn't have any. I could've made millions." He looked over his shoulder into the dining room where the remains of his Christmas dinner now lay cold. "I had found it," he said in a quiet voice. "I was just getting ready to celebrate, when"— Talbot looked at Mother—"when you came to the door." He slit his eyes and lips. "You pushed your way in so quickly when you heard the cats. I had to stop you, I was so close."

"And just what did you think you'd do with me, Bernard?" Mother challenged, venturing closer.

"I don't know. Reason with you?"

"You grabbed me and tied me up!" Mother retorted. "How would I reason with that?"

A tear welled in Talbot's eye. "I was so close."

I had been so engrossed in Talbot's tale that I hadn't heard the sirens approach. The police had arrived.

While I remained watchful of Talbot, fireplace poker at the ready, Mother opened the front door to let the police in. She explained the situation and they arrested him. As they set up their crime scene paraphernalia and questioned us, Chewy and Sorceress rested at my feet, the turkey feast putting them to sleep.

"I had come over to see if Talbot had seen Beamer

when I heard him crying in the back," Mother told the sergeant in charge. (Apparently her hearing was far better than mine, for I hadn't heard any cats until I had entered the cattery.) "I pushed past him to get Beamer. Talbot grabbed me and tied me up. When Margo knocked on the door"—she glanced at me—"he shoved me into the back room. You know it from there, Margo."

As Mother went to fetch her cat, I filled in the rest of the story. Talbot was handcuffed, a heavy jacket draped over his shoulders, and taken to the patrol car.

I took Mother and Beamer home, placing my exhausted cats in the SUV where they could sleep peacefully. I called my husband to fill him in on what had happened. He suggested that I invite her to our house for dinner and to spend the night. She turned us down.

"I have other things to do," she retorted.

"Ah, so you do celebrate Christmas, Mother!"

Her face flushed red with embarrassment. "In the true sense of the purpose, Margo. Christmas isn't about big meals, presents, or decorations. That's just a government plot to help boost the economy during a slow season. It's about giving. Fulfilling the needs of others."

I smiled and shook my head.

"Come, Margo." She took my arm, dragging me behind her out the door. "We've got work to do. Now."

We returned to Doctor Talbot's house, now swarming with police and reporters. Mother convinced the officer in charge, whom she happened to know, that all they needed was to take some photos and DNA samples from the cages, releasing the cats to her. We loaded the frightened felines into the back of my SUV. The noise didn't wake the Bengals. They were in a turkey divine dreamland. Chewy snored, his head tucked against Sorceress's neck.

We drove through the night, from house to house, bringing joy to all the people who had thought they'd lost their furry loved ones forever; much like the fabled Santa Claus brought toys to the children of the world. Only, our sleigh was pulled by horsepower instead of reindeer power and filled with the chorus of felines instead of angels.

We finished delivering the "presents" at sunrise on Christmas Day. I returned Mother to her house and lay beside her on her bed, exhausted, Beamer a purring ball on her legs.

"You know, Mom," I breathed, my eyes closing, "I'm still learning from you. Merry Christmas."

She took my hand in her own and we slept.

Excerpt from *Rest in Pieces*

RITA MAE BROWN AND SNEAKY PIE BROWN

Christmas Eve morning dawned silver gray. The snow danced down, covering bushes, buildings, and cars, which were already blurred into soft, fantastic shapes. The radio stations interrupted their broadcasts for weather bulletins and then returned to "God Rest Ye Merry Gentlemen." A fantastic sense of quiet enshrouded everything.

When Harry turned out Tomahawk and Gin Fizz, the horses stood for a long time, staring at the snowfall. Then old Gin kicked up her heels and romped through the snow like a filly.

Chores followed. Harry picked up Tucker while Mrs. Murphy reclined around her neck. She waded through the snow. A snow shovel leaned against the back porch door. Harry put the animals, protesting, into the house and then turned to the odious task of shoveling. If she waited until the snow stopped she'd heave twice as much snow. Better to shovel at intervals than to tackle it later, because the weather report promised another two feet. The path to the barn seemed a mile long. In actuality it was about one hundred yards.

"Let me out. Let me out," Tucker yapped.

Mrs. Murphy sat in the kitchen window. *"Come on, Mom, we can take the cold."*

Harry relented and they scampered out onto the path she had cleared. When they tried to go beyond that, the results were comical. Mrs. Murphy would sink in way over her depth and then leap up and forward with a little cap of snow on her striped head. Tucker charged ahead like a snowplow. She soon tired of that and decided to stay behind Harry. The snow, shoveled and packed, crunched under her pads.

Mrs. Murphy, shooting upward, called out, *"Wiener, wiener! Tucker is a wiener!"*

"You think you're so hot," Tucker grumbled.

Now the tiger cat turned somersaults, throwing up clots of snow. She'd bat at the little balls, then chase them.

Leaping upward, she tossed them up between her paws. Her energy fatigued Tucker while making Harry laugh.

"Yahoo!" Mrs. Murphy called out, the sheer joy of the moment intoxicating.

"Miss Puss, you ought to be in the circus." Harry threw a little snowball up in the air for her to catch.

"Yeah, the freak show," Tucker growled. She hated to be outdone.

Simon appeared, peeping under the barn door. *"You all are noisy today."*

Harry, bent over her shovel, did not yet notice the bright eyes and the pink nose sticking out from under the door. As it was, she was only halfway to her goal, and the snow was getting heavier and heavier.

"No work today." Mrs. Murphy landed head-deep in the snow after another gravity-defying leap.

"Think Harry will make Christmas cookies or pour syrup in the snow?" Simon wondered. *"Mrs. MacGregor was the best about the syrup, you know."*

"Don't count on it," Tucker yelled from behind Harry, *"but she got you a Christmas present. Bet she brings it out tomorrow morning, along with the presents for the horses."*

"Those horses are so stupid. Think they'll even notice?" Simon

criticized the grazing animals. He nourished similar prejudices against cattle and sheep. *"What'd she get me?"*

"Can't tell. That's cheating." Mrs. Murphy decided to sit in the snow for a moment to catch her breath.

"Where are you, Murph?" Tucker always became anxious if she couldn't see her best friend and constant tormentor.

"Hiding."

"She's off to your left, Tucker, and I bet she's going to bust through the snow and scare you," Simon warned.

Too late, because Mrs. Murphy did just that and both Tucker and Harry jumped.

"Gotcha!" The cat swirled and shot out of the path again.

"That girl's getting mental," Tucker told Harry, who wasn't listening.

Harry finally noticed Simon. "Merry Christmas Eve, little fellow."

Simon ducked away, then stuck his head out again. *"Uh, Merry Christmas, Harry."* He then said to Mrs. Murphy, who made it to the barn door, *"It unnerves me talking to humans. But it makes her so happy."*

A deep rumble alerted Simon. *"See you, Murphy."* He hurried back down the aisle, up the ladder, and across the loft to his nest. Murphy, curious, stuck her head out of the barn door. A shiny new Ford Explorer, metallic hunter green with an accent stripe and, better yet, a snow blade on the front, pulled into the driveway. A neat path had been cleared.

Blair Bainbridge opened his window. "Hey, Harry, out of the way. I'll do that."

Before she could reply, he quickly plowed a walkway to the barn.

He cut the motor and stepped out. "Nifty, huh?"

"It's beautiful." Harry rubbed her hand over the hood, which was ornamented with a galloping horse. Very expensive.

"It's beautiful and it's your chariot for the day with me as your driver. I know you don't have four-wheel drive and I bet you've got presents to deliver, so go get them and let's do it."

Harry, Mrs. Murphy, and Tucker spent the rest of the morning dropping off presents for Susan Tucker and her family, Mrs. Hogendobber, Reverend Jones and Carol, Market and Pewter, and finally Cynthia Cooper. Harry was gratified to discover they all had gifts for her too. Every year the friends exchanged gifts and every year Harry was surprised that they remembered her.

Christmas agreed with Blair. He enjoyed the music,

the decorations, the anticipation on children's faces. By tacit agreement Cabell would not be discussed until after Christmas. So as Blair accompanied Harry, the cat, and the dog into various houses, people marveled at the white Christmas, and at the holiday bow tied on Tucker's collar, compliments of Susan. Eggnog would be offered, whiskey sours, tea, and coffee. Cookies would be passed around in the shapes of trees and bells and angels, covered with red or green sparkles. This Christmas there were as many fruitcakes as Claxton, Georgia, could produce, plus the homemade variety drowning in rum. Cold turkey for sandwiches, cornbread, cranberry sauce, sweet potato pie, and mince pie would be safely stowed in Tupperware containers and given to Harry, since her culinary deficiencies were well known to her friends.

After dropping off Cynthia's present, they would drive through the snow to the SPCA, for Harry always left gifts there. The sheriff's office was gorged with presents, but not for Rick or Cynthia. These were "suspicious" gifts. Cynthia was grateful for her nonsuspicious one.

Blair remarked, "You're a lucky woman, Harry."

"Why?"

"Because you have true friends. And not just because

the back of the car is crammed with gifts." He slowed. "Is this the turn?"

"Yes. The hill's not much of a grade but in this weather nothing is easy."

They motored up the hill and took a right down the little lane leading to the SPCA. Fair's truck was parked there.

"Still want to go in?"

"Sure." She ignored the implication. "The doors are probably locked anyway."

Together they unloaded cases of cat and dog food. As they carted their burden to the door, Fair opened it and they stepped inside.

"Merry Christmas." He gave Harry a kiss on the cheek.

"Merry Christmas." She returned it.

"Where is everybody?" Blair inquired.

"Oh, they go home early on Christmas Eve. I stopped by to check a dog hit by a car. He didn't make it." Harry knew that Fair never could get used to losing an animal. Although he was an equine vet, he, like other veterinarians, donated his services to the SPCA. Every Christmas during their marriage, Harry brought food, so Fair naturally took those days to work at the shelter.

"Sorry." Harry meant it.

"Come here and look." He led them over to a carton. Inside were two little kittens. One was gray with a white bib and white paws and the other was a dark calico. The poor creatures were crying piteously. "Some jerk left them here. They were pretty cold and hungry by the time I arrived. I think they'll make it, though. I checked them over and gave them their shots, first series. No mites, which is a miracle, and no fleas. Too cold for that. Scared to death, of course."

"Will you fill out the paperwork?" Harry asked Fair.

"Sure."

She reached into the carton and picked up a kitten in each hand. Then she put them into Blair's arms. "Blair, this is the only love that money can buy. I can't think of anything I'd rather give you for Christmas."

The gray kitten had already closed her eyes and was purring. The calico, not yet won over, examined Blair's face.

"Say yes." Fair had his pen poised over the SPCA adoption forms. If he was surprised by Harry's gesture, he wasn't saying so.

"Yes." He smiled. "Now what am I going to call these companions?"

"Christmas names?" Fair suggested.

"Well, I guess I could call the gray one Noel, and the

calico Jingle Bells. I'm not very good at naming things."

"That's perfect." Harry beamed.

On the way home Harry held the carton on her lap. The kittens fell asleep. Mrs. Murphy poked her head over the side and made an ungenerous comment. She soon went to sleep herself. The cat had eaten turkey at every stop. She must have gobbled up half a bird all totaled.

Tucker took advantage of Mrs. Murphy's food-induced slumber to give Blair the full benefit of her many opinions. *"A dog is more useful, Blair. You really ought to get a dog that can protect you and keep rats out of the barn too. After all, we're loyal and good-natured and easy to keep. You can housebreak a corgi puppy in a week or two,"* she lied.

Blair patted her head. Tucker chattered some more until she, too, fell asleep.

Harry could recall less stressful Christmases than this one. Christmases filled with youth and promise, parties and laughter, but she could not remember giving a gift that made her so blissfully happy.

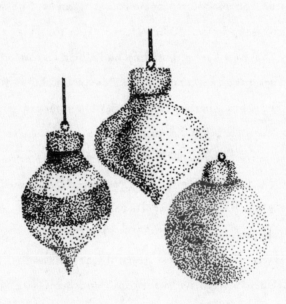

Letter to Louise, Part III: Being the Meditations of Midnight Louie in New York City from *Cat in a Golden Garland: A Midnight Louie Mystery*

CAROLE NELSON DOUGLAS

I am about to impart to you some priceless wisdom, just in case you are my daughter and could use some guidance. Being priceless, wisdom is no doubt undervalued, but here I go anyway: the best place to be on Christmas Eve, I have discovered, is the kitchen. That is where all the eats are, and where the noise level is the least.

"I have unwittingly spent many a Christmas holiday out-of-doors, aware only that there were a good many more turkey leavings outside my favorite restaurants during the season to be merry. Also, the handouts came with a tad more mercy, but not noticeably so.

"Now I have seen the light. Or, rather, I have seen lots of lights. It is fitting that I am spending my first indoor Christmas in Manhattan, which becomes an island of illumination for the period. The small twinkling lights Miss Temple Barr adores (perhaps because she is more than somewhat small and twinkling herself) bedeck the city's stern gray-granite face like electrified fleas on a dignified Russian Blue grand champion. (I pity these purebreds; they are never allowed to have any fun. There is something to be said for being relatively worthless in the scheme of things.)

"I understood that humans became merry and bright at such a time, but admit that either quality is in short supply around Miss Kit Carlson's domicile this Yuletide. I should report my progress in investigating murder most foul, in the high-rise atmosphere of a Madison Avenue advertising agency, the very place where I am a VIP (Very Important Pussycat). A man playing Santa

Claus (he of the red long johns and white curly whiskers) became entangled in a length of golden chain while exiting the traditional chimney at the company Christmas party. It turns out the Santa who was hung by the chimney with care was an actor-type acquaintance of Miss Kit Carlson.

"So she has decided to move her Christmas Eve party to the day after the holiday in deference to Rudy's death, as he was known to most of her acquaintanceship as well. The festivity will instead be a farewell party for Miss Temple—for myself and Miss Temple, I might point out, were there anybody sensible to point it out to. By then, Miss Kit says, there may be something to really celebrate, such as Miss Temple's and my elevation to feline spokespersons. Or the solution to Rudy's bizarre death.

"Still, Christmas cannot go unheralded. Food is casual but in ample supply, and often left out on the countertop for a little Midnight noshing. Miss Kit has installed a small fir tree atop a living room table and twined it with fairy lights and other glittery folderol. Certain packages wrapped in gaudy paper and ribbon lie beneath it. I even detect an odor of exotic catnip beneath the pervasive stench of pine tree, but try to ignore it, as surprise seems to be a highly valued commodity at these Christmas festivities. (Although the suspense of Santa never emerging from the chimney was not one of those valued surprises.)

"Needless to say, the spokescat search at said advertising agency has ground to a halt, not only for the holiday itself, but until your old man . . . I mean your elder maybe-relative . . . solves the manner, motive and mastermind of Rudy's death, which of course is murder in the first degree. So there is no rest for the hunter of wickedness, not even on Christmas Eve. I suspect I will join my ladies in lounging around and sighing, although I will not be joining them on their Christmas Day outing to St. Patrick's Cathedral, where something known as high mass is to be celebrated.

" 'I am not even Catholic,' I hear Miss Temple protest lukewarmly.

" 'You never know,' Miss Kit responds with that mock severity she is so good at. 'And it never hurts to be well rounded, just in case. Besides, sectarian religious concerns aside, it is glorious theater, and the music makes the latest Andrew Lloyd Webber Broadway smash seem modest.'

"So I will be alone by the phone on Christmas Day, at least for a while, twiddling my shivs while waiting impatiently for my gift weed to cure for a few days longer. It seems present-opening is to be delayed by Rudy's death as well. I do not think the dead dude would begrudge me a little holiday nip, given his own lifelong proclivities, but must abide by others' sense of propriety, which is never as liberal as my own. Since I do not drink . . . wine, I have plenty of time to leave the ladies to their holiday blues and French reds in the living room and retreat to the computer.

"I find myself in a contemplative mood as I face great changes in my lifestyle and the specter of future fame and fortune (though my fortune will be tied up with the affairs of others and certainly cannot be lavished willy-nilly on remote relatives). Perhaps it is time to let bygones be bygones. I see now that my job as house detective at the Crystal Phoenix hotel was a mere stepping stone to greater things, so it is your world now, and welcome to it.

"Now that I have been altered beyond my wildest

dreams (and also have seen dozens of human offspring in mass holiday revelry at the advertising agency), I must admit that your headstrong hieing to the veterinarian for spaying was perhaps not a bad decision for a career woman like yourself. From what I hear, you are doing a good job at keeping the ruder elements in line at the Crystal Phoenix. All in all, you are not a bad kit—though by no means mine beyond a shadow of a doubt; I am no deadbeat dad, only cautious—and in the spirit of this season that seems to mean so much to humans, I offer you an olive branch (or even some of my imported nip, should I ever get it).

"And you could do worse than to consult now and again with your esteemed grand—er, grand friend, Three O'Clock Louie, who has traveled widely and seen much of the world that even I might be a tad ignorant of.

"So let us hope that Bastet blesses all of catkind this season, every one, and even a few deserving humans.

"I am sending this whole e-mail file to Miss Van Von Rhine's office, trusting that she will see it gets to the proper party. She is pretty smart for a human. I am

in such a mood of reconciliation that I even send
Chinese New Year greetings to Chef Song, and fond
wishes that his koi remain in the best of health until I
get back.

"Yours in news, nip and nostalgia,
Midnight Louie, Esq."

The Noel Cat

SHIRLEY ROUSSEAU MURPHY

*W*hen Virgie Woods saw that stray cat slinking through the muddy snow, she was so angry with life that she felt nothing more for the thin, starving waif than for a fly on the wall. Not that she'd hurt it, or any living creature—except maybe her worthless brother. Hector Lee deserved a clout on the head or whatever else he got in life. And of course she had no human love for that Worley clan, the young smart-ass hoods who killed her Muffy. Her anger at the world, after Muffy's death, was so overwhelming that it was all she could do to check out books and get through the library's story hours trying to keep her reading voice cheerful and the little kids laughing. Muffy had been the official Greeley Library cat. When he died so terribly, the kids nearly rioted with rage. If Hector Lee'd been here, that day, to watch the library, those Worley boys—surely high on some drug—wouldn't have scooped Muffy up, the little yellow cat being so trusting with everyone . . .

Leaning over her desk to look out the library window, Virgie felt a shiver of hopelessness, watching the stray cat out in the mud and snow. A white and orange cat, what she could see under the mud that caked its coat. When Virgie moved behind the glass, the cat sprang away and vanished into the bushes.

She waited until it crept out again warily, its stomach dragging. Clearly it was nursing kittens. Crouched in a muddy puddle, it peered out at Main Street as if wanting to race across; it went rigid when it heard a noise in the bushes behind it, and it was gone again. Virgie peered through the window into the bushy shadows, sickened by the cat's thin, bony body under that dirty, matted coat. Despite her bitterness, if that cat was hurt or sick, she knew she'd have to do something about it.

She didn't want to be involved with another cat. Sure not a starving stray and a bunch of sickly kittens. She listened guiltily to the choir down at the church practicing Christmas carols; this holy season, she should be in a more charitable frame of mind. Seemed there was nothing kind left inside her, only anger.

A voice in her head said, That little cat has no one, Virgie. But Virgie didn't want to listen. Her hurt over Muffy's death was a hard lump in her, and seemed all to center on Hector Lee. If he'd just been there in the library that day. Hector Lee was just worthless. He might have abandoned the petty crimes of his youth, but he sure hadn't straightened up. Never had a steady job. And too hardheaded to come live there in the cottage behind the library with her, as a proper brother should in their old age. . . .

Even as she sat thinking about Hector Lee, she saw him going into the jail up the street carrying his bedroll, his backpack slung over his shoulder. Moving in for the coldest part of the winter. Moving in to mooch off the sheriff and the town. Their sheriff was too good natured. From half a block away she could see Hector Lee's week's growth of beard, his muddy shoes and stained, wrinkled khaki pants. Her own brother, choosing to spend the winter in jail.

Though Greeley jail *was* usually empty, and was better shelter than that windy shack out by the quarry, that was no more than a chicken coop. Sheriff never used those old cells anymore unless the new county jail was full. But why didn't Hector Lee find the gumption to fix up his own place? Clean himself up, too. Shave, try to get a steady job instead of a few odd jobs when the mood took him.

When the cat appeared again, creeping and shivering, she knew it had lived its whole miserable life in a panic of fear and hunger. Well, the cat didn't have a choice. Hector Lee had a choice. Shuddering, Virgie turned away. There were stray cats all over Greeley, wild cats that refused to be tamed; and half-wild farm cats that lived fine on mice and rats. Folks in Greeley believed that if you fed a mouser it wouldn't hunt. That without hungry stray cats, the rats would come right out of the woods and overrun the town. Well it was true Greeley's old brick buildings, the courthouse and stores and library, had plenty of holes in the foundations where mice and rats liked to invade; buildings dating from the war between the states; the library and her little cottage went back to the time of Sherman's march through Farley County burning and killing. When she dug her bit of garden in the spring, to plant her vegetables, she would find hand-cast lead balls from their old muzzle loaders.

Somehow Sherman had missed burning Greeley. Folks told some wild stories about that; some said Greeley had just vanished from the map until Sherman passed on by, headed for Atlanta, then the town appeared again, to keep on fighting the north. Some said the stray cats around Greeley had all appeared at that time, so many stray cats all with bright orange eyes the color of Sherman's fires.

Well, this *was* a southern town; its stories were cherished, as they should be. A wealth of southern folklore passed down the generations; that was why southern literature was so rich, Virgie thought—southern children sitting on the porches listening to their elders' tales, generation after generation, growing up to tell their own stories.

Virgie's life as Greeley's librarian was more a labor of love than a living. Oh, she had her social security, and the little old cottage the town provided was rent free. Four rooms just behind the library, small and dingy but cozy enough. Every few years the women of the library board got someone to paint it for her, but the paint never did much good, the dark stains of smoke from the woodstove bled right through again.

Beneath the window the cat started away across the yard, its belly dragging the trampled snow. Where were her kittens? Virgie wondered if that big old tomcat had killed them. Maybe that was why she was so nervous. So much killing, at Christmas time. That tomcat—biggest cat she'd ever seen, hanging around real bold, not staying out in the woods like most of the wild ones. Most all tomcats would kill kittens. Virgie stared up at the ceiling as if she could see right through to the sky and to the face of her maker, wondering why He had, in His infinite wisdom, made tomcats to kill innocent kittens?

But she knew why.

"Away in a Manger" rang along Main Street, the choir's sweet voices lifting Virgie up for a moment, reaching in to ease her anger. It was less than a week until Christmas. She remembered the Italian legend about one little kitten born under Christ's manger, and she thought about putting out some scraps for this poor mama. How could that mama cat hunt for food when it was weak from hunger and from nursing kittens? Virgie imagined those kittens—if they were still alive—their little pansy faces . . .

After Muffy died, and the town's children settled down from their tears and shouting, they had brought a succession of farm kittens around to the library hoping she'd take a shine to one, that they'd have another library cat. She'd shaken her head, and turned them all away.

But Muffy had had a good life, eighteen years coddled and loved by the whole town. It was a badge of achievement, in this backwoods town, for a cat to live right in the library among the books. Well, it was a badge of achievement for Greeley to *have* a library. Except, this was the county seat. Muffy had been petted by her readers and fed tidbits by the children; it was special indeed for a cat to be mourned in a long procession of village children and buried, with a headstone, in the library garden.

Below her, the cat seemed easier now. It sat down in the mud and began to wash. Watching it with a strange, unwanted longing, Virgie shook herself. The morning was getting on, it was almost ten, time to open up. Saturdays were busy with children checking out books.

In his cell, Hector Lee folded the jail blanket neatly at the foot of the cot next to his bedroll. He liked this corner cell, it was the biggest, and was nice and light. The warmest, too, being right under the overhead heat vent. Sheriff would let him keep it unless county jail got full and they sent over a bunch of no goods. Then Sheriff'd move men in with him. He hated that, hated sharing with young, smart-ass studs. If it came to that, he'd move back out to his shack beside the quarry even if it was cold enough to freeze the balls off a bull. His old board shack, no matter how much scrap wood he nailed on the sides or how much scrap he burnt in the woodstove, scrap he toted from the sawmill that they'd throwed away, it was cold as a frozen outhouse. He looked down the short hall between the three cells and the office. At the end of the hall, over the clock, Sheriff had put up a couple branches of white pine decorated with red paper bells. Down the street, the choir was practicing . . . *Oh come ye, oh come ye, to Bethlehem.* . . .

On Christmas Day, Hector Lee knew, Virgie would bring him a fine dinner; he always looked forward to that. Turkey, stuffing, mashed potatoes and gravy and cranberries, all the makings. And a whole, big, homemade punkin' pie just for him. Oh, his sister could cook, even if she was a librarian and so stiff and proper. Pie so good, made you think you'd died and went to heaven.

Well, it felt real good to tuck up in his old cell. He'd made it legal, so not to get Sheriff in trouble, had stole half a dozen cans of beans from the corner market, enough to get arrested proper. Sheriff never locked Hector Lee's cell door. He could still go out to do odd jobs, if it weren't too cold, shovel snow from folks' walks, and the like. Lookin' out his barred window he could see Virgie at the library window; she'd be lookin' over here cluck-clucking because he'd moved into his old cell for the winter.

Except, she wasn't lookin' over to the jail, she was leaning over, her forehead against the glass, peering down at the muddy ground. At first, he couldn't make out what she was looking at. Then something moved—a skinny cat, sitting in the mud washing its paws. Seemed like a waste of time washing paws that would be muddy again the minute the cat set them down. But then the cat stopped washing, and looked around toward the bushes.

And there, toddling unsteadily out to press against the cat, was a might of a kitten.

The mama cat looked to be orange with white mark-ings, what you could see under the mud. Kitten, though, it was bright orange and white and black, pretty as a hound pup.

Was there only the one kitten? He couldn't see no more hiding in the bushes. Likely that ole tomcat had got 'em. So *that* was why it'd been hanging around: kill the kits, get the female to come back in heat. Big old battered tomcat the color of scrub water. He'd seen it outside the courthouse and in the alley turning over garbage cans, strong and bold as a dog, seen it snatch food from the trash behind the diner. Seen it tear up a couple of pet cats, too, and attack Miss Millie Severn's little lap dog. He heard that Millie'd loaded her husband's shotgun and swore she'd kill the beast. That tomcat didn't look to be a critter a person'd want to get friendly with, great big dirty white cat with brownish streaks, head as wide as a road scraper. Orange eyes that blazed at a person like lightning flash.

He watched Virgie come out of the library door with a bowl in her hand and kneel down in the snow a few yards from the crouching female and its kit. That was Virgie, couldn't resist mothering a stray. His sister had a giving heart—too giving. Bake him pies, then try to lure him to living all proper in that cottage with her, smothered like a beast in a cage. The shadows were growing heavy, starting to get dark; dusk came quick in the winter. Virgie was very still, watching the thin cat and its kit.

Well, that cat weren't about to come to her, she should know that. Them wild ones, you couldn't get near 'em. When the cat didn't move but only stared at the food, Virgie finally set the bowl down, rose, and went back up the steps and inside. Hector Lee shook his head. Too bad. Virgie, all unknowing, had set a trap for that cat. That wild mother was foolish to let down her guard, to be distracted by a human. Tomcat would drive her off, kill the kit, and, for good measure, take the supper Virgie'd left. Hector Lee watched 'till it was too dark to see. Turned away when Sheriff brought him his own supper, a burger and fries from the diner. Sheriff was as portly as his three deputies, his uniform tight across his belly, from good eating; though his face was sharp planed and determined; Hector'd seen him take down a few mean ones with a single, hard blow. Sheriff handed him the Styrofoam box. "Surprised Virgie didn't bring you a bowl of bean soup, Hector Lee, this cold night."

"I expect she doesn't know I'm here, yet," Hector Lee said, seeing Virgie's shadow at the dark library window again, still looking out at the stray cats. Hardly touching his burger, he searched the darkness for the tomcat, feeling his heart quicken. Tomcat mean as a human killer out there stalking that helpless female and her kit.

Virgie might call him worthless, but he had a tender spot or two—not that he liked to show Virgie. He watched until it was too dark to see. Over at the church, the choir was practicing, *Noel, Noel. . . .*

Turning from the bars, Hector Lee tied into his cooling burger and fries, wishing he had a double chocolate malted. He finished quickly, stuffed his napkin into the Styrofoam box, shoved it out onto the hall floor, and curled up in his bedroll warm and comfortable. He liked the feel of solid brick walls around him, sure didn't miss the icy wind whipping through the cracks of his own thin wooden walls. In the quiet jail, serenaded by Christmas carols, Hector Lee slept.

He slept thus for three nights, peaceful and long, his thin belly filled with burgers and fries, and then, when Virgie knew he was there, her good beef stew and apple pie, and then her Brunswick stew and pecan pie and ice cream. No matter how she disapproved of the way he lived, he was her brother, her only family, and she relished doing for him. Each night when she appeared at the jail, pulling open the cell door and handing him his supper, she'd tell him about the little cat and kit.

"They're coming up the porch steps now, Hector Lee.

After dark. They're eating from the bowl right there on the top step. Remember our cats, when we were kids? Remember we had a little calico, a lot like this little kit?"

He remembered. He thought there was no need to mention the tomcat that was prowling, no need to distress her. He didn't understand why that cat had, so far, left those two alone. Maybe it was afraid to go so near the house, but that seemed strange, bold as it was. Hector Lee, rolled in his bedroll thinking about them cats, felt real peaceful hearing Christmas carols fill the dark. That music warmed him with a happy haze that embarrassed him, for its soft foolishness.

By the end of the week, Virgie said she'd enticed that mama cat and kit right up on the porch beside the rocking chairs. Hector Lee said, "Then that ain't no wild stray, Virgie, somewhere along, that cat's lived with folks."

"Whatever the case," Virgie said stubbornly, "I'm set on taming them."

Hector Lee thought he might ought to tell her about the tomcat; but he didn't. They were sitting on the bunk in his cell, Virgie pretending to be at ease there. "There's only the one kit, surely. That's all the mama ever brings, Hector Lee. Just that one bright orange and black and white princess." Virgie laughed. "That's how I think of her. And that little kit's eyes, they're as big and green as emeralds."

Well, Hector Lee thought, the tomcat had stayed away so far. Maybe it had gone off somewhere, maybe the mother cat and her kit would stay lucky.

It was the fifth night, just after Virgie had taken Hector Lee over a plate of baked pork chops and apple dumpling and sat with him for a while in the chill cell that, coming home, the cat and kit followed her up her steps and right on inside her cottage. She was afraid of frightening them; but when she opened the door, hardly breathing, they followed her right on in, never made a bobble, just plopped down on the rug and looked up at her. She swallowed, and stepped to the kitchen alcove, leaving the front door cracked open so the cat wouldn't feel trapped. She cut up her pork chop that she'd kept warm in the pan, blew on it until it cooled, and put it on a plate on the rug.

When the mama and baby both began to gobble bits of pork chop, Virgie sat down at the table and ate her plate of dumplings. The cats finished eating and curled up together on the rug, the kitten falling deeply asleep as if it was exhausted, the mama jerking awake every few minutes, at any smallest sound from out beyond the front door. Virgie stayed at the table for nearly an hour, reluctant to move and frighten them. She rose at last, did up the dishes as quietly as she could. Only when she tried closing the door, did the cat panic. Quickly she opened it again, pushed in a stout shoe to keep it open, and fixed the burglar chain in place. That chain wouldn't keep anyone out, but the little town didn't have much theft. Crime in Greeley revolved around bigger issues: pot farms hidden back in the hills because there wasn't much call for moonshine anymore; drug smuggling coming through their little county airport headed for dealers in Atlanta. Matters that wouldn't have to do with an unlocked cottage door. Besides, with the sheriff just up the street, she felt safe enough. Putting on her flannel gown, Virgie went to bed. Heavy frost covered her windows.

She got up twice during the night to look into the living room where the cats still slept, curled together. The third time she woke, the cat was up and pacing, staring at the window. Not until it settled down again, did Virgie go back to bed. It was that night while Virgie slept that, across at the jail, Sheriff roused Hector Lee from sleep.

The time, by the jailhouse clock, was three A.M. Before Hector Lee knew what was happening, Sheriff shoved three men into his cell, and slammed and locked the door. Sheriff stood for a minute looking in. "I'm sorry, Hector Lee. You can sure come on out, right now. Can go on home, or over to Virgie's for the night, maybe."

Hector Lee looked at the young, half-drunk, belligerent Worley brothers slumped on the other three bunks. Rod and Jude scowled. Randy Worley was tense and angry, glaring at Hector Lee hungering for a fight. Old Hayden Worley's boys. Mean as snakes. Across the hall, the other two cells held two Worley cousins, and an uncle and a second cousin. Hector Lee looked over his three cellmates, and knew he'd be smart to leave. But, waked up in the middle of the night by this scum, he felt as mean and contrary as the Worleys looked. "I'll stay here, Sheriff."

"Come on out of there, Hector Lee."

Stubbornly Hector Lee sat down on his bedroll. Sheriff gave him a look, touched his side arm as if to force Hector Lee out, but then he scowled and turned away. Randy Worley waited until the sheriff had gone on into his office, then he jerked Hector Lee off his bunk. "You'll sleep on the floor, old man."

"You don't need my bunk, Randy."

Randy stretched out on Hector Lee's bedroll and yawned. Hector Lee jerked him up and got in two hard punches before Randy had him down, beating on him.

He woke on a cot in the sheriff's office, his jaw and eye hurting bad. His side felt like raw meat. When he moved, that pained him so, he hoped a rib weren't broke. He must have moaned, because Sheriff turned in his swivel chair. "How you feel, Hector Lee?"

"I've been better." Shivering, he looked up at the barred office window. The dawn light was cold and gray.

"There's a glass of water there on the file cabinet, Hector Lee. And some aspirin." Sheriff rose and shook out three aspirin for him, handed them to him with the water. Leaning painfully up on one elbow, Hector Lee swallowed them down.

"Try to get some sleep," Sheriff said. "I don't . . ." The phone rang and he turned back to the desk. Hector Lee rolled over real careful facing the wall where the light wasn't in his eyes, and pulled the blanket up. He meant to go back to sleep but the sheriff's conversation held him listening.

". . . plane must have landed around midnight. One

of my deputies lives out there but was on duty. Got home around one, the plane was tied down, the field empty. He'd passed the boys' car on the road. He called in, and took off after them. Half an hour before we found them. Not a thing in the car, they've stashed it somewhere. Deputies are out looking. If you have a drug dog free, to send up here . . ." Sheriff listened, and made a grunting sound in his throat. "Well, hell. Guess that's more important." He listened again, then, "If these punks *won't* talk, and we don't have the stash by noon I'll call you, see if you can pull a dog off for two or three hours."

He listened, then, "Well, yeah, a lot of farms and open country, but they didn't have time to go far. This isn't a very big town, maybe we'll get lucky."

Sheriff's last words before he hung up the phone were disgust that his jail was full of scum on Christmas Eve morning. Hector Lee was drifting off when the sheriff left the jail. He heard him talking with a deputy, then heard the front door slam. His dreams were filled with the hurts he'd been dealt, and, strangely, with the sweet voices of the Greeley choir—as if the two elements were engaged in some fierce battle. He woke with the sun in his eyes through the barred window, and the Worley boys banging their shoes on the bars shouting for breakfast. A deputy, sitting at the desk, looked around at Hector Lee. His thin black hair was slicked back, pink scalp showing through, his cheeks pink from shaving. "You going on back to your place, Hector Lee? You can't move into the office for the winter," he said, grinning.

Hector Lee didn't answer.

"Calling for more snow. By tonight, temperature'll be down around zero." Deputy watched him. "It's Christmas Eve morning, Hector Lee. You could sleep in Virgie's garage for a few nights, until we can make room in county jail for those punks."

Hector Lee swung off the cot. "You fetching some breakfast for those snakes?" he asked hopefully.

The deputy laughed, and rose. "Ham and eggs?" Hector Lee nodded. He was rolling up his bedroll, and the deputy not back yet with breakfast, when Virgie came for him.

"I need you to come help me, Hector Lee. It's the little cat, the stray. There's a tomcat started hanging around. I'm afraid he's set to kill the kitten. I thought maybe you could . . . maybe trap it? Or borrow a shotgun? A big, mean-looking tomcat, all scarred up from fighting and killing."

Hector Lee said nothing, just stood looking out the window waiting for the deputy, listening to his stomach growl.

"Hector Lee? I have bacon in the skillet and sourdough pancakes . . ."

Hector Lee looked at Virgie. Well, he might could go on over there, just for a bit of breakfast.

He followed Virgie through the snow and mud thinking about her good sourdough pancakes slathered with molasses. But he sure didn't want to shoot no tomcat. Heading around behind the library to her cottage, Virgie said, "Cat wanted to go out this morning. Real insistent, guess she wanted to hunt. Herded her kit right out, I couldn't keep them in. Maybe she's back now, she . . . there," she said, pulling him back.

In the shadows by the door, the cat and kit were crouched and watchful. Hector Lee stood still as Virgie went on up the steps like nothin' was different. But before she could reach for the knob, the cat looked past her at Hector Lee and was gone, her kit beside her. Hitting the end of the porch they disappeared around the side of the house, among the bushes.

Virgie looked back at him helplessly, both of them thinking of the tomcat. He followed her in through the house and sat down at the kitchen table. She cooked his pancakes, distracted, kept looking out the window. Hector said, "Cat won't come, with a stranger here. I'd best . . ."

"She'll come," Virgie said. "Be patient. Eat your breakfast." She looked at Hector Lee. "Jail's full of those Worleys, Hector Lee. They killed my Muffy. Oh, I hate that family. They're dangerous. And it's too cold for you to go back to your place, you don't want to freeze to death all alone, on Christmas Eve."

Hector Lee grinned at that. Virgie said no more; and before he knew it, they were outside again, bundled up, looking for the mama cat and her kit. "Maybe she'll come to the house while we're gone," Virgie said. "Maybe I can come back alone and get her inside."

Hector Lee followed her wondering what he was doing out in the muddy snow freezing his tail looking for stray cats. "Twice last week," Virgie said, "I saw them go in the garage. You stay here, let me have a look." She went in through the side door and shut it, so the cat wouldn't run out. Hector Lee didn't know what good that would do, the garage door didn't fit tight, you could drag a steer under that door. He stood shivering in the snow, his boots wet, his feet freezing, his mind filled with cold thoughts. How much need a fellow do, just to earn breakfast? He could hear her inside, moving stuff. If them cats were in there, that would chase them out. He waited for near ten minutes, then Virgie opened the door a crack. "Come in quick, they're in here somewhere, I heard a rustling and a little thump."

Inside, he could see three clean squares in the dust of the cement floor, over in the corner where she'd moved some boxes. "Put your hand in here behind these other boxes, Hector Lee, these rags back in here are warm. They must've been sleeping here when I opened the door. She might even have born her kittens here."

He looked behind the boxes, reached in and felt the dirty rags. They were warm, all right, and smelled of young animals. Virgie said, "I guess she's been coming in here all along. Maybe that tomcat is too skittish to come inside. I'd best put those boxes back, or she'll be really upset." The boxes she'd moved were neatly labeled: Old towels. Cancelled checks. Turkey roaster. He remembered family dinners when they were kids, a twenty-five-pound turkey sizzling brown in that roaster. Virgie didn't have cause no more to cook a big turkey dinner. Undoing the four flaps of a box lid, she looked in at packets of bank statements and cancelled checks held together with rubber bands. "Years old. These can go in the fireplace."

But then, frowning, she lifted out a canvas bag from beside the bales of checks. "I don't . . ." A sound made them turn.

The tomcat stood in the middle of the garage, looking at them. He did not look friendly. If he'd been any bigger, a fellow would want to back off. Virgie had opened her mouth to say something, when the female appeared on the shelf above the tom, looking down at him. Everyone was still. Then the mama cat jumped down, chirruped to her kitten, and the two of them waltzed past the tomcat, not inches from him; sauntering to the corner, they leaped over the boxes and settled down in their nest. The tomcat sat looking after them, his body and tail softly relaxed, his purr loud and ragged. Virgie smiled.

"I never," Virgie said softly. "That's his little family. Not a tomcat in a thousand would do like that." Satisfied that the tomcat meant no harm, she set the canvas bag on the workbench and opened it, frowning at a tumble of small plastic bags.

"Rock salt," Virgie said. "But we haven't made ice cream . . ." Her eyes widened.

"Not rock salt," Hector Lee said softly, looking at the stash. "Better open the rest of them cartons . . . No, second thought, better not."

⊰•⊷•○•⊶•⊱

Twenty minutes later Virgie had the female cat and her kit inside the house, settled down with a bowl of cat food. She had just picked them both up from their nest, real bold and gentle like, and carried them right out, before the sheriff and four deputies arrived to take pictures and lift fingerprints and count the bags of crack. Leaving the law to their work, and with the state drug unit on the way, Virgie and Hector Lee sat at her kitchen table drinking coffee, eating her good punkin' pie, watching the two cats settle in, and listening to the choir's sweet voices, *Hark! the Herald Angels.* . . . The tomcat had disappeared.

Tomcat showed up again hours later, when the law had finished in the garage and gone away. It was just dusk. Outside, all was quiet, no music now. Already folk were heading for the church. Soon most of Greeley would be crowding in for the service—there would be grand music, then. It was truly Christmas Eve; and when they looked out the window, there stood the tomcat, staring in at them.

Handing the kit to Hector Lee, and picking up the mama cat in her arms, Virgie opened the door. She let him see the female, then she stood aside.

Tomcat, he looked up at the scrawny little female, and he looked at Virgie. And without a by-your-leave he walked up onto the porch past Virgie as bold as Sherman himself, and right on into the house. Followed Virgie and the little female right on into the kitchen where Virgie poured him a saucer of cream off the top of the milk jug. Fresh thick cream.

That was the way the mama cat and her kit and that ole tomcat moved in with Virgie. And that cat, he helped the mama take care of their kit and teach it to hunt, as gentle as a person could want. Virgie said, "I guess, once in a while, you find a tomcat like that." Hector Lee, he moved in, too, into Virgie's spare bedroom. All of a sudden Virgie Woods wasn't alone anymore. And, it being Christmas Eve and all, Virgie thought that was the way a southern story should end. With family coming in out of the cold together, the spicy smell of Christmas baking, the turkey roaster waiting all scrubbed to take a fresh turkey, and holy music filling the night brighter than Sherman's fires ever blazed.

As for them Worley boys, there was no Christmas Eve charity for that bunch. The DEA boys packed 'em off to Atlanta, and no one in Greeley, that Christmas Eve nor ever after, was sorry to see them go.

Kitty "Box"-ing Day

Betsy Stowe

Christmas is the time of year
When humans go insane—
Rushing, wrapping, hiding gear,
And never time for games.

They bring trees right inside the house
But never let us climb,
Hang shiny, dangling objects out
We're not supposed to find!

So cats must make our own good fun,
Ignoring normal rules,
And claiming for our own the one
Thing cast aside by fools!

Paper, boxes, bags, and bows—
Amusement park for cats!
To shred, to hide, to take a roll
Sounds like a mousie's scratch!

Colored, crackly paper sheets . . .
I must untie this knot!
This pile was once a single piece.
My kingdom for a box!

Then finally attention runs
Back to its rightful place.
Festivities are overcome
By my too gorgeous face!

I make them laugh. 'Don't even care
That they forgot my treat.
Admit it, felines have the flair
To make Christmas complete.

The Mystery of Musetta's Mistletoe

CLEA SIMON

istletoe? No, Musetta! Put it down!" Even as I jerked awake, startled from sleep by the thud of my stout pet landing on the pillow beside me, my cat-loving instincts kicked in. "Put that down, Musetta!"

The round green eyes staring at me were all innocence as I reached for her, but she dropped the sprig. The muted green leaves and white berries had started alarms in my head—mistletoe may not be fatal to cats, but who wanted to deal with even a moderately sick feline during the crazy season? Only when I picked it up did the last of the cobwebs clear: It was plastic, a false alarm.

"Musetta? Where did you get this?" She was

grooming, stretched around to a hard-to-reach place at the small of her glossy black back, and didn't respond. "Kitty?" She straightened up and stared back at me, but only licked her pink nose.

"Strange." I twirled the plastic plant in my hand. I sure hadn't brought it into the apartment we two shared, not being a fan of fake plants or of Christmas, particularly this year. Musetta reached a white mitten out to bat at the faux sprig, and I made her stand up for it, exposing her fluffy white belly.

"Tickles!" I yelled, giving in to the urge to ruffle her soft tummy fur. My vulnerable pet nipped me for my troubles and then jumped off the bed, leaving me with the plastic mistletoe. Fake cheer. How appropriate, I thought, my mind racing back to the night before.

That was supposed to be fun, too. A holiday party, hosted by one of my friends, but Bill—my sometime boyfriend—and I had arrived already snarling. The evening hadn't started that way. Sitting up in bed, I could still see the five outfits I'd discarded in my quest for a perfect party look, and the stretch velvet dress I'd chosen— olive green to set off my red hair—now lay draped over my bedside chair.

The problem was the holidays, the whole "be jolly" spirit. That was what had urged me to push Bill. To ask him again for a key to his place, to make us more of a real couple. I'd reached for an excuse: "It will match the one I gave you when you had to sit Musetta last month." But we both knew what I was doing. So when he hesitated— beginning one of those "Theda, aren't we having fun?" speeches every woman knows—I'd pulled back and snapped at him. A hurt look had flashed over his face, but his response was curt, and everything had just gone downhill from there. By the time we reached our destination, we might as well have been at different parties. I talked to my friends; he moped, his tall, lean frame wedged into a corner. I danced, he glowered, particularly when a string of slow songs found me in the arms of a particularly hunky guitarist. Maybe I was being a jerk. Some of that dancing was awfully close. But didn't Bill deserve it? Yeah, he gave me a ride home, but that was it; his long face had been closed and stern. The guitarist—what was his name? Dan? Dave?—hadn't even asked for my number. And so I'd tossed and turned in my favorite ugly flannels, and now, to add to it all, my cat was acting weird.

"Musetta? Don't you love me?" She knew better than to respond to emotional blackmail and I had to get out of bed to find her, sitting by the window. I turned my back on her and shuffled into my tiny kitchenette. Coffee helped lift the funk somewhat, as did a heaping bowl of Raisin Bran: comfort food for the terminally single. But when I turned on the radio all I could find was holiday music—Christmas songs, actually—and there was nothing festive about my mood.

Still, there were gifts to purchase—for myself anyway—and cat food to be bought, so I cut short my perusal of the Sunday paper and gave in to the luxury of a long shower. Indoor plumbing—now that was something to celebrate. On a whim, I let the tub fill, too, squeezing in my favorite bubbles. Without Bill in the picture, who cared how pickled my skin got?

Just as my eyes closed and I felt myself sliding into the warm, fragrant foam, something touched my face. Something leathery and cool, and just a little grainy.

"Musetta?" Opening my mouth had been a mistake. The paw had batted at my moving lips, and I sputtered out what I truly hoped was not kitty litter. Those big green eyes were staring at me again, and in her mouth I saw a ribbon.

"Kitty!" This was getting exasperating. How can one cat find so many dangerous toys? Water slopped over the side sent her scurrying, but not before I'd grabbed the offending length of green ribbon. As I held it up, I saw a pair of small silver bells tied to its end. No wonder she'd been tempted—anything bright caught my cat's attention—but that didn't answer the basic question: Where had she found this? I'd not started wrapping anything yet, and knowing what ribbon or string of any kind can do to a cat's insides, I kept all my decorative bits of yarn and the like in closed drawers.

"Musetta? Where did this come from?" She returned to the bathroom doorway, a safe distance from the offensive wetness on the floor, but eyed the tiny bells longingly. I raised them and shook. They jingled. She advanced and soon, puddle or no, we were engaged in a game of kill the bells, which lasted until my bathwater cooled.

"Mistletoe, Musetta? Jingle bells?" Even as I dried and dressed, I couldn't make sense of this and sought out my pet, who was lounging again on the windowsill, where the midday sun would warm her dark back. "What's with the Christmas stuff, anyway?"

She yawned and looked out the window. Clearly I was boring her. I shook the little bells. She glanced back at me and blinked. Maybe it was the green of her eyes, maybe it was the slightly bored, aloof expression, but for a moment she reminded me of Bill. Almost ten years older than me, he did tend to act above it all. Just like a cat at times. Musetta turned away. I snapped.

"You know, young lady, we don't celebrate Christmas in this house. We don't sing carols. We don't have a tree. And we don't keep mistletoe and jingle bells around." I knew I was getting worked up about nothing, but all the feelings from last night had come flooding back. I shoved the beribboned bells into my pocket and turned on the bored cat. "Christmas is just one more winter solstice holiday and a Christian one at that. Well, okay, maybe the mistletoe is pagan. But unless we're going to start observing all the holidays, and that means Kwanzaa too, then there'll be no more Christmas in this house! Our last name is Krakow—we're Theda and Musetta Krakow, kitty. We're Jewish. Or, well, I'm Jewish and I'm your mother, so that makes you a Jew, too. And we celebrate Chanukah. It's all well and good to mesh customs when we're getting along with our

Christian friends . . ." An image of Bill's warm green eyes, his lazy smile, passed through my head. "But when it's just us two, then I'm not going to let you bury our identity in the mass-marketing and the tinsel and everything."

I was being too loud: With one annoyed look, Musetta jumped down from her sunny perch and retreated under the sofa. How could I blame her? My outburst hadn't made me feel any better either. I needed to get out of the house.

For someone with an attitude toward the holidays, Harvard Square was the wrong place to be. Brightly colored tinsel twined up the lampposts, and the free-form stars outlined by tiny white lights on the banners that crossed Massachusetts Avenue could be made out even in broad daylight. Some student group had gotten itself up in a rough approximation of Dickensian costume to sing carols, nearly blocking the entrance to my favorite bookstore. And down the road, in front of the pharmacy where they carried my one essential winter moisturizer, even the regular street musician, an avuncular accordionist, was picking out what could have been "Good King Wenceslas."

"Hey, babe!" He smiled and nodded, unwilling to leave off his wheezy carol for a wave.

"Grrr . . ." I responded and then, feeling guilty, dug out a dollar to put in his instrument case.

"Merry Christmas, beautiful!" I ducked into a storefront before I said something I'd regret, and only when my temper settled down did I realize that I'd opened the wrong door. This wasn't the pharmacy, it was the stationer's shop next door. But it was warm, and there's something calming about paper and writing supplies. I had no appointments, I could browse.

And there I saw it: The pen. With its blue-marbled barrel and fine gold nib, this was the fountain pen Bill had been lusting for only a week before. That day had been a happy one. We'd come into the Square for brunch and then window-shopped, enjoying the cacophony of the holiday crowds and the street entertainers who'd braved the frigid weather. I'd needed a cartridge for my printer, then, and we'd ended up in this same store. I'd worried that Bill would be bored, but as I finished up my purchase in the back, I'd seen him talking to one of the clerks, who then removed the same smooth leather case from the window.

Conklin, was it? Or Conway? I didn't remember, only that at the time I'd stayed back as Bill had taken the pen, reverentially, in two hands. The clerk had offered to fill it, to let him try it out, but Bill had handed it back.

"No thanks," I could hear his voice in my head, a little sad with longing. "It would be wasted on me. I don't need it."

The real shop swam in front of me as my eyes filled with tears.

"May I help you?" A voice at my shoulder brought me back.

"Yes, may I see that pen, please? The blue one?"

"The Conway. Great choice. It's restored, but near mint condition, and a really great price."

Before I could think about it, I'd pulled out my Visa. "Do you gift wrap?"

"Of course."

What was I thinking? I didn't even know if I'd see Bill again. But what the hell. It was a beautiful object, a piece of art. Maybe I'd learn to love fountain pens, too.

For no discernible reason, my mood was lifting. I lucked into a sale on my moisturizer and some other goodies as well, which helped, and turned my face up to the sun's scant warmth as I made my way back home. Maybe Bill and I could make up. Maybe these December days were the darkest we'd see all year.

The shadows were lengthening as I turned up my block and climbed the steps to my old brick building. "Hey, Theda!" The super was wrestling the big trash bins out front for the morning pickup. "Happy holidays!"

"Hi, Roman! Good solstice to you, too!" He was probably just angling for a tip, but who cared? Two flights of stairs and I'd be home. Would Musetta have any more mystery presents for me? An image of a gift-wrapped mouse appeared in my head and I chuckled as I reached for my keys.

The laugh died in my throat. There was a movement ahead, up the stairs, right by my door. A dark shadow—a man's coat?—had slipped inside.

"Roman?" As in a nightmare, my voice came out in a whisper. "Roman?" But he was outside, I knew, no help, and certainly not the reason my door stood slightly ajar.

I should have left then. Should have run back out

to the street and yelled for the burly super, for my neighbors, for the cops. But too much had happened in the last twenty-four hours, and I was sick of it. Sick of feeling rejected and put upon, of having one good mood after another dashed by the unexpected. I picked up the pharmacy bag. With its jumbo tube of Aveda and the economy-sized shampoo—also on sale— it would make a decent weapon. With my other hand, I slammed my apartment door open and prepared to swing.

"Theda!" A man in black knelt by my door.

"Bill?" Those green eyes, his black wool coat. What was he doing on my floor?

"Rrow!" I dropped the heavy bag to the floor. My cat dived under the sofa.

"What are you doing here?" He was smiling now, a little sheepish.

"I was hoping to sneak one more surprise in for you." He held out his hand. There, on a length of thick red yarn, were two keys. I recognized the larger one; it fit the old front lock of his building. "They're a set. Your own set."

He stood. I looked up in his face, his kind, sweet face.

"You were right, Theda. I'm sorry I reacted as I did. Too many years alone, I guess." He took my hand and placed the keys in my palm, then covered my hand with his. The yarn was soft and fuzzy.

"Yarn?"

"That was meant for Musetta, actually. She's been so good about the other gifts." He took a can of catnip spray out of his coat pocket. "This helped."

"The mistletoe? The jingle bells?"

"I still have your keys, remember? Unless you really want me to, I'm not giving them back." Suddenly we were both laughing, the mystery of the mistletoe solved, and I was able to explain the basics of cat care—and cat safety—to Bill, who took my little lecture in good grace. By the time the "no ribbon, no string" rule had been explained, we were able to coax Musetta out from her hiding place so she could join us for a snack while we made plans for dinner.

"I wanted to show you that my holiday could be intimate, too. That it didn't all have to be commercialized and overblown," said my Bill, once the three of us were nestled on the couch. "I wanted it to be fun."

"It will be," I said to his collar, as I cuddled into his

shoulder and Musetta kneaded the pillow beside me. "Christmas and Chanukah both." Out in the foyer, under the bag of toiletries, I had the perfect present, and it was already wrapped. If only I could get Musetta to deliver it. . . .

Holiday Safety

CHRISTINE CHURCH

ecember 24th was always a special night for the Fergusons. The Christmas tree glistened in splendor, glass bulbs of various colors twinkled, multi-colored lights bounced from the shining surface of the glass ornaments. And lambent light from the silver tinsel created a rainbow for the eyes as the tinsel hung in excess from each branch.

It was all so magnificent and beautiful to behold. And quite enticing, particularly for the Ferguson's cat, Missy, a short-haired brown tabby born, it seemed, with a twinkle of mischief in her eye. All that movement, all that intrigue. She reached a paw toward an especially low-hanging bulb.

"Missy!"

Missy replaced her paw to the ground and turned her head. She understood her name, and when spoken in such a manner, she knew that meant to stop whatever she was doing, or risk getting hit with the water sprayer. With a yawn and a sigh, Missy rested beneath the tree instead and napped, dreaming of those enticing wonders above her.

When she awoke, her people were gone. The house was dark. They had gone out for the evening. Light from a street lamp shone in and illuminated a bulb on the tree. It appeared to twirl and circle. No one home. No one to say "no."

The cat reached a paw and sent the shiny ball spinning. Another bat and it swung back and forth, back and forth.

But on the third good swing, something unexpected happened. The ball flew from the tree and made a loud noise on the hard wood floor, crashing, smashing into pieces.

The pieces twinkled, but didn't move. Curious, Missy sought them out, trying to play with one, but the pain in her paw made this no longer a fun endeavor.

She licked the small cut and returned to the tree. So many more interesting sights! Long thin silver strands hung from each branch.

Pulling them from the tree was simple. What more could a kitten want? Long and stringy and shiny!

Hours later, the Fergusons arrived back home. Mrs. Ferguson gasped as she turned on the den lights to find a disaster. The tree was torn apart; tinsel littered the floor, broken balls and ornaments everywhere. She yelled for Missy, but the cat did not come. The family started a search.

Eventually she was found curled under a spare room bed. She did not look comfortable at all. As a matter of fact, their little cat appeared quite ill. A rush to the vet and X-rays revealed she had ingested several strands of tinsel and some stringed popcorn, which had wadded in her stomach and wrapped around her intestines. She would need surgery.

The next few days were touch and go, but the Fergusons, and Missy, were lucky. The kitten recovered fully, and her family learned a valuable lesson; be careful with holiday ornaments around a curious kitten.

Holiday Fun

The holidays, especially Christmas, with all its lights and sparkling wonders, is a joyous time, and can be "the most wonderful time of the year," to quote a classic song. It can also be one of the most dangerous to a curious cat or kitten. And there are many reasons this can be. More than simply the enticement of a luminous Christmas tree.

The Present

What could be more exciting than to receive a squirming and adorable kitten as a present? But then we must think about the cat's point of view. A small kitten may simply act with curiosity, an adult cat with fear. In either case, the last thing you want to do to your cat is to frighten her with excessive noise and interaction. And that's exactly what the holidays encompass. If you wish to give a cat as a gift, first be sure the recipient definitely wants this animal in his or her life. You do not want to throw a live animal onto someone who will not be prepared to care for it. If the gift is yours, then be sure you are prepared to care for the cat or kitten at a time when things are not as hectic.

Christmas Trees and Decorations

Christmas holds many fanciful sights and wonders, for a curious cat, and particularly for a kitten, whose world is still being discovered. It can also be one of the most dangerous holidays for a cat. Always keep a kitten's curiosity in mind when decorating. Breakable, toxic, or harmful ornaments, plants, and knickknacks should be kept out of the cat's reach or not used. Strings of popcorn or beads, as well as the string and needles to make these garlands, can kill your cat.

Electrical cords, if bitten into, can pose a fatal risk. Some cats love to chew them, bat at them, claw them. Keep your electrical cords bound tightly and wrapped in aluminum foil or another material that is unattractive to cats. Cords can also be run above doors, secured to the wall along baseboards, or in some other way fastened out of your pet's reach. Also be careful not to let cords run under furniture or carpets on a permanent basis, or the cord can get worn down after a time and cause a fire.

Another way to help keep your cat off the cords is to purchase from a pet supply store or veterinarian a product with a bitter taste that can be sprayed on electrical cords (or plants) to make them taste bad. However, this might not work as a one-time preventive measure if you have a particularly mouthy kitten or cat. And the taste will eventually wear off and have to be reapplied.

Fireplaces and kerosene heaters should be protected with safety screens. It is in your cat's best interest to err on the side of caution and make sure the cat cannot come into contact with or be exposed to hot embers or sparks. Wood-burning stoves usually pose little danger to cats, but some cats will sleep so close to the stove that their fur becomes hot to the touch.

Guests

And let's not forget the stress of all that new company coming in and out of the house. Cats are creatures of routine. Some are quite sociable and will welcome each new guest. Pounce is such a cat. He loves parties, for he can move from lap to lap, licking the noses of unsuspecting visitors. Other cats, however, will run and hide, refusing to come out until hours after the last person has vacated.

If you have indoor cats, be careful guests do not inadvertently let your cat out. Put up signs, and inform guests that your cats are not allowed outdoors; ask them to please be careful and close the doors well behind them. You might want to allow only one door to be opened and closed, thus eliminating the worry of more than one escape route for the cat(s). The Christmas snows are not the time you want to be searching for a lost kitty. If you can, supervise the door each time a guest arrives or departs.

If your pet will be happier, keep her locked away in another room, particularly one she finds comfortable, such as your bedroom where your scent is prominent. Be sure you provide your pet with enough food and water and a clean litter box to last until she is able to be released. Keep the door locked, or a No Entry sign posted clearly.

Holiday Foods and Alcohol

We love all the foods of the holidays: Christmas cakes, cookies, fruitcake, and plenty of other delicacies to tempt the palate. Your cat should not be tasting these treats along with you, even if she begs. Chocolate, especially, can make a cat very sick. In high enough quantities, it can be fatal, particularly to small kittens.

Potato chips and like snacks might not be fatal, but

should also be off-limits, or only allowed in very small quantities. The salt content is terribly high, and too much can cause a chubby tabby. Fortunately, most cats don't like human treats like chocolate and chips, but there are definitely exceptions.

Precious is one of these exceptions. She is a cute little nineteen-year-old Tortie who adores Doritos and other cheesy snacks. She is allowed a very tiny portion, only on rare occasions. If you have one of these junk food kitties, moderate any snacks, remember no chocolate, and be careful of quantities.

What would the holidays be without a holiday turkey or ham to add an enticing aroma to the air? Imagine that same aroma if you possessed 500 million olfactory nerves (as opposed to a human's 5 million)? Wow! How can any feline resist? But resist she should! Though it is all right to feed your kitty a few boneless scraps, please be careful where you dispose of the bones. They can splinter within the cats' digestive tract and cause ruptures that may be fatal.

And how humans love to indulge in a bit of the spirits during the holidays! But please keep Kitty out of these festive indulgences. Alcohol is quite toxic to cats. At the very least, it can make your beloved feline extremely ill.

Plants

We all adore the look of beautiful Christmas wreaths and flowers. But some can make your cat very ill, especially the most popular of those: poinsettia. Though not as toxic as once thought, they can still produce vomiting and diarrhea, which can lead to dehydration. In a small kitten or older cat, this can be fatal. It might be nice for us humans to sneak a kiss under the mistletoe, but the plant is deadly to cats. Some other plants to watch out for include: Christmas rose, holly, philodendron, and dieffenbachia. For a list of plants poisonous to cats, please visit: www.cfainc.org/articles/plants.html. If there is an emergency, you can call the Animal Poison Control Center at (888) 426-4435.

Love Thy Pet

And, last, but certainly not least, don't forget to love your pet during this special occasion. This can be a very hectic time of year with guests, family, cooking, wrapping, and shopping. But in the midst of all the hustle and bustle, Kitty still needs your attention. Now more than ever is a time to celebrate not only the season, but the love and joy that your cat brings to your heart!

The Purr-fection of Christmas Ritual

WENDY CHRISTENSEN

ey, Mom, come quick, you gotta see this! Two snowplow guys are fighting out in the road. One of 'em slid off the street into the wall and then the other guy showed up and hit two mailboxes and crashed into the first one, and then the one guy took off his gloves and threw 'em at the other guy, and both their hats fell off and . . ."

"Ryan! Go back outside, can't you see I'm busy?" Her chilly words freeze the boy's gush of words. "And take Jen with you. She's making too much noise with that game box of hers. I have to have these done by three-thirty."

From her perch on the window ledge, Moonflower raises her head and gazes, questioning and bemused, at the excited child and his overwrought parent. "Humans!" she seems to mutter to herself, though the only sound is her gentle purr. In a tiny, graceful, quintessentially feline ritual, she blinks three times, stretches one paw toward the sun, and returns to her feline dreams.

Snow-booted feet scamper, the door slams. For a moment, all is quiet. Then, in a sudden burst of guilt and worry, the beleaguered woman jumps up, runs to the door, flings it open, and shrieks, "And stay away from those plows!" Sighing, she goes back to the cluttered kitchen table, where she's hand-painting two dozen paper plates for the cookie exchange. Much as she'd like to, she can't skip this competitive annual neighborhood ritual—and its ritual obligations.

Oh, those obligations! The checklists, the gift lists, the to-do lists. The expectations, the guilt, the commitments, the compulsions, the burdens, the chores, the shopping. Finding a parking place at the mall. Baking twelve dozen cookies by Tuesday morning. Facing dreaded Mother-in-Law, and her perfectionist wrath, specially honed for inciting holiday stress and fear. And what if Uncle Bill gets drunk and disorderly at dinner again? The hype, the craziness, the expense—they get worse every year. But what can a mother do?

The answer is right in front of her, dozing and purring on the window ledge in the sunshine.

Christmas, at its best, is a timeless ritual recognition of human kinship, and of our deep connection with the rhythms of nature. By observing this mid-winter milestone, we join hands in an endless chain with our fellow humans, past, present, and future. As part of this great chain, we celebrate in faith, anticipate in hope, and honor with love and humility the return of the sun. Each year, our long-ago ancestors watched with alarm as the hours of daylight inexorably dwindled. With mounting disquiet and dread, they anxiously measured the times of light and darkness. Would the sun fade away forever this time? We can only imagine their relief and gladness when the decline stopped, and—very gradually—the daylight time started to, once again, lengthen. The winter solstice salutes the life-giving sun, and commemorates its unhurried but unmistakable return. Over the millennia, various religions have overlaid their own feasts and festivals on the ancient solstice observance, deepening its vitality and significance, layer by layer.

We humans need rituals like this, just as we need

stories, those universal narratives we repeat to each other and to ourselves, to help decode the mysteries and enigmas of life, the universe, and everything. Stories and rituals keep us grounded, connected, and sane. But here in the U.S., in the early twenty-first century, the rituals of Christmas have become a kind of ritual madness.

Cats, as anyone who has lived in their company knows, adore rituals. For such intelligent, curious, and adaptable animals, they're endearingly fond of their daily routines. But unlike humans, who tend to overload rituals until they collapse beneath the weight of expectation and disappointment, cats treasure the simple, cyclical daily-ness of life's routines. A special food bowl, filled at a particular time, in a certain place, by a familiar person who announces dinner with the same reassuring words and phrases, in the same loving tones—that, to a cat, is the most perfect of rituals. No hidden agendas, no point-scoring, no score-settling, no frills, no surfeit. Just ease, peace and grace, cheer, comfort, and sharing—curiously, just what Christmas is supposed to be.

"I'm just trying to create Christmas memories for my kids," wails frazzled Mom. (Frazzled, now there's a Christmassy word.) But what will Ryan and Jen really remember? Probably a cranky, snappish mother who was too busy with some silly project to relish the marvelously absurd spectacle of hatless snowplow drivers boxing without gloves on an icy road.

Such an unexpected bit of performance art is something that only a child, or a rare adult who's retained a childlike appreciation of absurdity, irony, and serendipity, can savor. People are fond of saying that they "do up" Christmas for their children, for the sake of creating memories. But memories can't be selectively "created"—not with the best of intentions, not with any amount of money. For a kid, the most enduring memories are zings out of the blue, ricocheting off the cozily familiar: the ritual of playing in the snow all day during vacation week, enlivened and rendered indelible by a small, unpredictable drama.

For Ryan, Christmas will eventually blur into an undifferentiated (if fond) haze of trees and lights, tinsel and glitz, wrapped packages and family dinners. But those battling snowplow drivers will live forever, in sharp and vivid detail. Too bad Mom missed it.

For too many of us, Christmas is no longer a celebration, but a relentlessly stressful, crazy-making jumble of the social, the commercial, the traditional, the religious, the personal—too many agendas, too much hype, too much of everything, slopped into a slender, sacred vessel never meant to contain such a potentially toxic brew. Impossibly overwhelming expectations and hopes are much too frequently squeezed into that One Big Day.

Merchants rely on Christmas spending as their chief engine of business success. Charitable organizations turn loose their slickest copywriters to fire up guilt and get those checks rolling in. Strife-torn families who should know better somehow talk themselves into believing that celebrating Christmas together will magically heal decades-old wounds, or at least paper over, with gaudy gift wrap, deep personal, religious, and political differences. Religious leaders try, with ever-declining success, to refocus attention on the holiday's spiritual aspects.

To a cat, though, Christmas is just another lovely day for her favorite rituals, spiced with a lively dash of the unexpected. Moonflower and her sister Rapunzel enjoy a long winter's nap on their sunny window ledge, their day punctuated by play, exploration, and extra snuggling time with their favorite people. The cats are delighted that

Ryan and Jennifer have been staying home all day instead of disappearing each morning. Even better, a real tree (maybe with real birds?) has magically taken root in the living room. Sparkly, blinking baubles dangle enticingly. Rapunzel, shall we climb? Yes, let's!

Do Moonflower and Rapunzel know that today is called "Christmas"? No, they do not. Would they care, if they did know? No, they would not. Naming a day cannot preserve a moment in time. There is no saving it, only living fully in that moment, tasting and smelling and touching and reveling in it. This moment, the eternal now, beckons eternally. There's that delightfully unexpected tree to be climbed, dangly sparkles to be batted, chased, pounced upon, demolished. And there may yet be birds in that tree!

If there's any agreement about Christmas, it's that it's all about gifts. On one hand, this obsession is a big part of modern Christmas's binge-and-burden mentality. But look more closely. Blink three times. Let the word tickle your whiskers. Extend a curious paw and tap its deeper meaning. Is it a coincidence that another word for gift is "present"? The present moment, however astonishing or mundane, is the only moment we, any of us, have. It is our gift. Cats know this. Humans have forgotten. Who is the more intelligent species?

Perhaps it's time to accept the gifts of wisdom and good sense from our cats. Perhaps it's time to step back, decelerate, unplug, simplify, clarify. Let's get off this roller coaster of exertion, emotion, exhaustion, elation, and enervation that pretends to be a sacred mid-winter festival. Moonflower, Rapunzel, and their kin will happily teach us that it's okay to say "No!" to excess, "No!" to acquisition obsession, "No!" to compulsive, competitive shopping, "No!" to the caricature of itself modern Christmas has become.

Instead, if we pay attention, they'll show us how to celebrate a low-key, low-stress, back-to-basics, cat-friendly, cat-safe holiday. You *can* get off the competitive shopping treadmill. Parties are optional. Really! Think before accepting invitations: Do I really want to go out— or would I rather stay home with my family and enjoy a quiet evening?

Cats are polite animals—another lesson humans would do well to learn. As we accept their gifts of everyday peace, sense, and wisdom, we can reciprocate by devising creative ways to enable them to safely and fully share in the best of our holiday traditions and celebrations. It's so much healthier for all to ban dangerous foods, decorations, and plants from your home than to burden your holiday with more reasons to fret. Do you still feel dragooned by empty custom to serve particular foods and display particular decorations? Follow Moonflower's lead instead, and feel gloriously free to enjoy whatever you like.

The only downside to offering a resplendent Christmas tree-gymnasium—sturdy, firmly anchored to the ceiling and ornamented with soft and pretty baubles— is that you aren't small or agile enough to revel in this novel pleasure. But Rapunzel and Moonflower are sure you share their spirit of adventure, and would clamber up if you could, sending all those crocheted snowflakes, tiny knitted mittens, and paper chains flying.

Because cats are highly sensitive to stress in their people, simply refusing to buy into the commercial Christmas rat race will bring immediate benefits for human and feline alike. Keeping to normal schedules and household routines makes the season bright and balanced, mellow and mem-orable—a quiet celebration rather than a riotous, unsettling muddle. Remember: Despite how the glossy magazines would have it, Christmas isn't a decorating contest, a culinary competition, a test of financial one-upsmanship, or a social status derby. Overstimulation, frantic busyness, worry, and overeating can be disastrous to feline and human health—not to mention destructive of the very felicity and serenity the holidays, at their best, promise.

No—Christmas is a joyous festival of faith, hope, renewal, and connection. Since the dawn of time, like our ancestors, we greet the gradually returning light and warmth of the sun with joy, relief, and gratitude. The ancient Egyptians, the first humans to keep company with cats in their homes, saw, in the light glowing within their cats' eyes, the great god Ra, the sun himself. It's no wonder that the Egyptians elevated the cat into their pantheon of deities in the form of Bast, or Bastet, a goddess with the body of a woman and the head of a cat. Bast was goddess of all good things: wisdom, music, dancing, fertility, sensual pleasure, happiness, warmth, and basking in the sun. Bast, goddess of the Moon, held the fire of the sun in her eyes overnight, preserving its light and warmth for her people. The ancient Egyptian word for cat is "miu" or "mau"—which also means "light."

Those of us who share our lives with felines can glory in this light, in this small, graceful symbol of our deep connection with nature, right in our own homes. How lucky we are! We possess the secret antidote to the ritual madness that modern Christmas has become. We can see the light, if only we care, if only we take the time to look. The answer is right in front of us, dozing and purring on the window ledge in the sunshine.

A good-hearted, cat-loving lady of my acquaintance once told me one of the saddest Christmas stories I've ever heard. As a young married woman with very little money, she was about to celebrate her first Christmas with her new in-laws. She took up her crochet hook and knitting needles and fashioned slippers, doilies, hats, and scarves. Her gifts were met with withering scorn: Too cheap to buy real gifts; Happy Hands at Home. This puzzled her. In the home in which she grew up, where cats were welcome and handmade gifts treasured, a prized Christmas tradition was the reading of "The Gift of the Magi." In that classic Christmas story by O. Henry, a penniless young wife sells her long, beautiful hair so she can buy her beloved husband an elegant platinum fob for his heirloom watch. Meanwhile, he sells his watch so he can buy her a set of tortoiseshell combs with jeweled rims—perfect for her glorious long hair.

Like O. Henry's young couple, cats don't stint, don't calculate, don't hold back. They don't hide their gifts on a high closet shelf, saving them for some future Christmas that might never come. They never fret that their gifts will be deemed unworthy. A gift is a creation of the moment, of the eternal now. The purr, the snuggle, the fond head-butt, the dead mouse, the soggy favorite toy . . . these gifts are ours now, right now. Give what you have, say our cats, generously and from your heart—and do it right now.

Cats aren't burdened by fears of being inadequate in the sight of their mothers-in-law, or of disappointing the neighborhood cookie mandarins. They're not in thrall to holiday clichés or stereotypes. They feel no obligation to conform to anyone's expectations. They're not tormented by guilt or regret, or psychologically paralyzed by trying to "create memories" or resurrect the supposed perfections of childhood Christmases.

Christmas and every other day, a cat lives in the blessed, eternal now. As the wise, cat-loving Ray Bradbury writes in *Dandelion Wine*: "You're in the present, you're trapped in a young now or an old now, but there is no other now to be seen." We humans see all those other nows, those Christmases of the past, those idealized, impossibly perfect Christmases, those Christmases that never were. We compare and contrast, we regret and worry. We stay up nights, fitfully fretting about the Christmases to come—the obligations, the expectations, all those lists. Our cats don't. They simply live in each day, each moment. Each day, Christmas or not, is a splendid new gift to be pounced upon, savored, relished.

Welcome Christmas with a swelling heart and swelling purr, not with dread and obsession. Relish Christmas as it was meant to be, in reverence, in humility, in gratitude, in bliss.

God Rest Ye Merry, Kitty Cats

(SUNG TO THE TUNE OF "GOD REST YE
MERRY GENTLEMEN")

LAURIE LOUGHLIN

God rest ye merry, kitty cats,

Let nothing you dismay.

Remember, lots of yummy food

Is served on Christmas Day,

To save us all from hungry tummies,

Hip, hip, hip hooray!

Oooh, tidings of catnip and joy,

Catnip and joy.

Oooh, tidings of catnip and joy.

Buster the Feline Retriever

JAMES HERRIOT

Christmas will never go by without my remembering a certain little cat. I first saw her when I was called to see one of Mrs. Ainsworth's dogs, and I looked in some surprise at the furry black creature sitting before the fire.

"I didn't know you had a cat," I said.

The lady smiled. "We haven't, this is Debbie."

"Debbie?"

"Yes, at least that's what we call her. She's a stray. Comes here two or three times a week and we give her some food. I don't know where she lives but I believe she spends a lot of her time around one of the farms along the road."

"Do you ever get the feeling that she wants to stay with you?"

"No." Mrs. Ainsworth shook her head. "She's a timid little thing. Just creeps in, has some food, then flits away. There's something so appealing about her but she doesn't seem to want to let me or anybody into her life."

I looked again at the little cat. "But she isn't just having food today."

"That's right. It's a funny thing but every now and again she slips through here into the lounge and sits by the fire for a few minutes. It's as though she was giving herself a treat."

"Yes . . . I see what you mean." There was no doubt there was something unusual in the attitude of the little animal. She was sitting bolt upright on the thick rug which lay before the fireplace in which the coals glowed and flamed. She made no effort to curl up or wash herself or do anything other than gaze quietly ahead. And there was something in the dusty black of her coat, the half-wild scrawny look of her, that gave me a clue. This was a special event in her life, a rare and wonderful thing; she was lapping up a comfort undreamed of in her daily existence.

As I watched she turned, crept soundlessly from the room and was gone.

"That's always the way with Debbie," Mrs. Ainsworth

laughed. "She never stays more than ten minutes or so, then she's off."

She was a plumpish, pleasant-faced woman in her forties and the kind of client veterinary surgeons dream of: well off, generous, and the owner of three cosseted basset hounds. And it only needed the habitually mournful expressions of one of the dogs to deepen a little and I was round there posthaste. Today one of the bassets had raised its paw and scratched its ear a couple of times and that was enough to send its mistress scurrying to the phone in great alarm.

So my visits to the Ainsworth home were frequent but undemanding, and I had ample opportunity to look out for the little cat which had intrigued me. On one occasion I spotted her nibbling daintily from a saucer at the kitchen door. As I watched she turned and almost floated on light footsteps into the hall, then through the lounge door.

The three bassets were already in residence, draped snoring on the fireside rug, but they seemed to be used to Debbie because two of them sniffed her in a bored manner and the third merely cocked a sleepy eye at her before flopping back on the rich pile.

Debbie sat among them in her usual posture: upright, intent, gazing absorbedly into the glowing coals. This time I tried to make friends with her. I approached her carefully but she leaned away as I stretched out my hand. However, by patient wheedling and soft talk I managed to touch her and gently stroked her cheek with one finger. There was a moment when she responded by putting her head on one side and rubbing back against my hand but soon she was ready to leave. Once outside the house she darted quickly along the road, then through a gap in a hedge, and the last I saw was the little black figure flitting over the rain-swept grass of a field.

"I wonder where she goes," I murmured half to myself.

Mrs. Ainsworth appeared at my elbow. "That's something we've never been able to find out."

It must have been nearly three months before I heard from Mrs. Ainsworth, and in fact I had begun to wonder at the bassets' long symptomless run when she came on the phone.

It was Christmas morning and she was apologetic.

"Mr. Herriot, I'm so sorry to bother you today of all days. I should think you want a rest at Christmas like anybody else." But her natural politeness could not hide the distress in her voice.

"Please don't worry about that," I said. "Which one is it this time?"

"It's not one of the dogs. It's . . . Debbie."

"Debbie? She's at your house now?"

"Yes . . . but there's something wrong. Please come quickly."

Driving through the market place I thought again that Darrowby on Christmas Day was like Dickens come to life: the empty square with the snow thick on the cobbles and hanging from the eaves of the fretted lines of roofs; the shops closed and the coloured lights of the Christmas trees winking at the windows of the clustering houses, warmly inviting against the cold white bulk of the fells behind.

Mrs. Ainsworth's home was lavishly decorated with tinsel and holly, rows of drinks stood on the sideboard and the rich aroma of turkey and sage and onion stuffing wafted from the kitchen. But her eyes were full of pain as she led me through to the lounge.

Debbie was there all right, but this time everything was different. She wasn't sitting upright in her usual position; she was stretched quite motionless on her side, and huddled close to her lay a tiny black kitten.

I looked down in bewilderment. "What's happened here?"

"It's the strangest thing," Mrs. Ainsworth replied. "I haven't seen her for several weeks, and then she came in about two hours ago—sort of staggered into the kitchen, and she was carrying the kitten in her mouth. She took it through to the lounge and laid it on the rug and at first I was amused. But I could see all was not well because she sat as she usually does, but for a long time— over an hour—then she lay down like this and she hasn't moved."

I knelt on the rug and passed my hand over Debbie's neck and ribs. She was thinner than ever, her fur dirty and mud-caked. She did not resist as I gently opened her mouth. The tongue and mucous membranes were abnormally pale and the lips ice-cold against my fingers. When I pulled down her eyelid and saw the glazing eye a knell sounded in my mind.

I felt the abdomen with a grim certainty as to what I

would find and there was no surprise, only a dull sadness as my fingers closed around a hard solid mass. Terminal and hopeless. I put my stethoscope on her heart and listened to the increasingly faint, rapid beat, then I straightened up and sat on the rug looking sightlessly into the fireplace, feeling the warmth of the flames on my face.

Mrs. Ainsworth's voice seemed to come from afar. "Is she ill, Mr. Herriot?"

I hesitated. "Yes . . . yes, I'm afraid so. She has a malignant growth." I stood up. "There's absolutely nothing I can do. I'm sorry."

"Oh!" Her hand went to her mouth and she looked at me wide-eyed. When at last she spoke her voice trembled. "Well, you must put her to sleep immediately. It's the only thing to do. We can't let her suffer."

"Mrs. Ainsworth," I said, "there's no need. She's dying now—in a coma—far beyond suffering."

She turned quickly away from me and was very still as she fought with her emotions. Then she gave up the struggle and dropped on her knees beside Debbie.

"Oh, poor little thing!" she sobbed and stroked the cat's head again and again as the tears fell unchecked on the matted fur. "What she must have come through. I feel I ought to have done more for her."

For a few moments I was silent, feeling her sorrow, so discordant among the bright seasonal colours of this festive room. Then I spoke gently.

"Nobody could have done more than you," I said. "Nobody could have been kinder."

"But I'd have kept her here—in comfort. It must have been terrible out there in the cold when she was so desperately ill—I daren't think about it. And having kittens, too—I . . . I wonder how many she did have?"

I shrugged. "I don't suppose we'll ever know. Maybe just this one. It happens sometimes. And she brought it to you, didn't she?"

"Yes . . . that's right . . . she did . . . she did." Mrs. Ainsworth reached out and lifted the bedraggled black morsel. She smoothed her finger along the muddy fur and the tiny mouth opened in a soundless miaow. "Isn't it strange? She was dying and she brought her kitten here. And on Christmas Day."

I bent and put my hand on Debbie's heart. There was no beat.

I looked up. "I'm afraid she's gone." I lifted the small

body, almost feather light, wrapped it in the sheet which had been spread on the rug and took it out to the car.

When I came back Mrs. Ainsworth was still stroking the kitten. The tears had dried on her cheeks and she was bright-eyed as she looked at me.

"I've never had a cat before," she said.

I smiled. "Well, it looks as though you've got one now."

And she certainly had. That kitten grew rapidly into a sleek handsome cat with a boisterous nature which earned him the name of Buster. In every way he was the opposite to his timid little mother. Not for him the privations of the secret outdoor life; he stalked the rich carpets of the Ainsworth home like a king and the ornate collar he always wore added something more to his presence.

On my visits I watched his development with delight but the occasion which stays in my mind was the following Christmas Day, a year from his arrival.

I was out on my rounds as usual. I can't remember when I haven't had to work on Christmas Day because the animals have never got round to recognizing it as a holiday; but with the passage of the years the vague resentment I used to feel has been replaced by philosophical acceptance. After all, as I tramped around the hillside barns in the frosty air I was working up a better appetite for my turkey than all the millions lying in bed or slumped by the fire; and this was aided by the innumerable aperitifs I received from the hospitable farmers.

I was on my way home, bathed in a rosy glow. I had consumed several whiskies—the kind the inexpert Yorkshiremen pour as though it was ginger ale—and I had finished with a glass of old Mrs. Earnshaw's rhubarb wine which had seared its way straight to my toenails. I heard the cry as I was passing Mrs. Ainsworth's house.

"Merry Christmas, Mr. Herriot!" She was letting a visitor out of the front door and she waved to me gaily. "Come in and have a drink to warm you up."

I didn't need warming up but I pulled in to the kerb without hesitation. In the house there was all the festive cheer of last year and the same glorious whiff of sage and onion which set my gastric juices surging. But there was not the sorrow; there was Buster.

He was darting up to each of the dogs in turn, ears

pricked, eyes blazing with devilment, dabbing a paw at them, then streaking away.

Mrs. Ainsworth laughed. "You know, he plagues the life out of them. Gives them no peace."

She was right. To the bassets, Buster's arrival was rather like the intrusion of an irreverent outsider into an exclusive London club. For a long time they had led a life of measured grace: regular sedate walks with their mistress, superb food in ample quantities and long snoring sessions on the rugs and armchairs. Their days followed one upon another in unruffled calm. And then came Buster.

He was dancing up to the youngest dog again, sideways this time, head on one side, goading him. When he started boxing with both paws it was too much even for the basset. He dropped his dignity and rolled over with the cat in a brief wrestling match.

"I want to show you something." Mrs. Ainsworth lifted a hard rubber ball from the sideboard and went out to the garden, followed by Buster. She threw the ball across the lawn and the cat bounded after it over the frosted grass, the muscles rippling under the black sheen of his coat. He seized the ball in his teeth, brought it back to his mistress, dropped it at her feet and waited expectantly. She threw it and he brought it back again.

I gasped incredulously. A feline retriever!

The bassets looked on disdainfully. Nothing would ever have induced *them* to chase a ball, but Buster did it again and again as though he would never tire of it.

Mrs. Ainsworth turned to me. "Have you ever seen anything like that?"

"No," I replied. "I never have. He is a most remarkable cat."

She snatched Buster from his play and we went back into the house where she held him close to her face, laughing as the big cat purred and arched himself ecstatically against her cheek.

Looking at him, a picture of health and contentment, my mind went back to his mother. Was it too much to think that that dying little creature with the last of her strength had carried her kitten to the only haven of comfort and warmth she had ever known in the hope that it would be cared for there? Maybe it was.

But it seemed I wasn't the only one with such fancies. Mrs. Ainsworth turned to me and though she was smiling her eyes were wistful.

"Debbie would be pleased," she said.

I nodded. "Yes, she would. . . . It was just a year ago today she brought him, wasn't it?"

"That's right." She hugged Buster to her again. "The best Christmas present I ever had."

About the Authors

Janine Adams is a lifelong lover of cats. Her four-block walk home from elementary school was frequently delayed by her stopping to talk with cats along the way, much to her mother's consternation. The author of seven pet-related books, including *How to Say It to Your Cat*, she lives in St. Louis with her husband, Barry; orange tabby cat, Joe; and standard poodles, Pip and Kirby.

Beth Adelman is a certified feline behavior consultant and a publishing professional. Her award-winning feline behavior book, *Every Cat's Survival Guide to Living with a Neurotic Owner*, was published by Barnes & Noble Books in 2003. She is the former editor in chief of *Cats* magazine and *Dog World*, former managing editor of the *AKC Gazette*, and has won several awards from the Dog Writers Association of America and the Cat Writers' Association for her work.

Cleveland Amory wrote many highly successful books about animals, including *The Cat Who Came for Christmas*, *The Cat and the Curmudgeon*, and *The Best Cat Ever*, as well as such widely praised works of social history as *The Proper Bostonians*, *The Last Resorts*, and *Who Killed Society*? He founded the Fund for Animals in 1967.

Rita Mae Brown is the best-selling author of *Rubyfruit Jungle*, *In Her Day*, *Six of One*, *Southern Discomfort*, *Sudden Death*, *High Hearts*, *Bingo*, *Starting from Scratch*, *Venus Envy*, *Dolley*, *Riding Shotgun*, and *Rita Will*. An Emmy-nominated screenwriter and a poet, she lives in Afton, Virginia.

Sneaky Pie Brown, a tiger cat born somewhere in Albemarle County, Virginia, was discovered by Rita Mae Brown at her local SPCA.

Renie Burghardt is a freelance writer with credits in books such as *Chicken Soup for the Horse Lover's Soul*, *Chicken Soup for the Christian Family Soul*, *Chocolate for Women*, and others. She lives in the country with four cats and four dogs.

Wendy Christensen, cultural ailurologist, cat-herder, writer, and painter, shares her rural New Hampshire home with her husband, more than ten thousand books, and the nine magnificent felines who are her models, muses, constant companions, and dearest friends. Her latest book is *Outwitting Cats: Tips, Tricks, and Techniques for Persuading the Felines in Your Life That What YOU Want*

Is Also What THEY Want (Lyons Press, 2004).

Christine Church's first book, *Housecat: How to Keep Your Indoor Cat Sane and Sound* was first published in 1998 by Howell Book House. In 1999, this book became a best-seller in Great Britain. In 2001, TFH Publications published Christine's book *Indoor Cats*, which won the Iams Responsible Pet Ownership Award for that year. Christine's next book, also by TFH Publications, was *Your Outta Control Cat*, and her latest, which was released in February 2005, is the revised edition of her first book, *House Cat*. Chris also writes fantasy fiction.

Steve Dale writes the syndicated newspaper column "My Pet World" (Tribune Media Services) and he's a contributing editor at *USA Weekend*. He's the host of syndicated *Steve Dale's Pet World* (www.petworldradio.net) and *Pet Minute with Steve Dale*, as well as *Pet Central* on WGN Radio Chicago (www.wgnradio.com). Steve is the editor in chief of *PawPrints*, a newsletter distributed to veterinarians around the world (in conjunction with Merial and the AVMA). He has set up the Ricky Fund at the Winn Feline Foundation to further research in feline medicine. To learn more, contact www.winnfelinehealth.org or call (732) 528-9797.

Carole Nelson Douglas is the award-winning author

of the Midnight Louie series, including *Cat in a Flamingo Fedora*, *Cat with an Emerald Eye*, *Cat in a Diamond Dazzle*, and *Cat in a Crimson Haze*. She lives in Fort Worth, Texas.

Jim Edgar lives in Seattle, where he runs the Web site www.mycathatesyou.com and muses the plight of the modern-day feline. He has also written the humor book *Bad Cat*.

Miriam Fields-Babineau is a designer of dog training products and the author of two novels, twenty-eight books about dogs and dog training, and one book on cat training. She resides in Virginia with her husband, son, two dogs, four cats, and horse.

James Herriot was born in Scotland and practiced veterinary medicine in Yorkshire, England, for half a century until he died in 1995. He is the author of *Every Living Thing*, *James Herriot's Cat Stories*, and *James Herriot's Dog Stories*.

Laurie Loughlin works in the medical field in Nashville, Tennessee, and parodies songs in her spare time. She has two cats, Greta and Penelope.

Willie Morris was the author of *My Cat Spit McGee*, *My Dog Skip*, *North Toward Home*, *New York Days*, and many other books.

Shirley Rousseau Murphy is the creator of the feline sleuth Joe Grey, P.I. in the mystery series beginning with *Cat on the Edge*, set in a small village on the California coast; of the cat fantasy *The Catswold Portal*, set in a world beneath San Francisco; and of earlier fantasies for children and young adults. She has been a painter and sculptor, a commercial artist and interior designer. She and her husband live in California with two lady cats, both rescued strays who enjoy all the amenities of a pampered life. Her Web site is www.joegrey.com.

Amy D. Shojai is an animal behavior consultant, award-winning author, lecturer, and a nationally known authority on pet care and behavior. She is a passionate proponent of owner education in her books, articles, columns, and media appearances, and can be reached through www.shojai.com. Her most recent books include *PETiquette: Solving Behavior Problems in Your Multi-pet Household* and *Chicken Soup for the Cat Lover's Soul*.

Clea Simon is the author of several books, including *The Feline Mystique* and the Theda Krakow mystery *Mew Is for Murder*. She can be reached through her Web site, www.CleaSimon.com.

Betsy Stowe is the author of *Calico Tales and Others* (Infinity), which has won five international awards, including the 2004 World's Best Cat Litter™-ary Award and a Muse Medallion™ from the Cat Writers' Association. The book is a loving collection of more than fifty of her cat poems and photographs.

Credits and Permissions

A Note from the Publisher

The seven-week-old kitten featured on this book's cover was found by our cover photographer at a local animal shelter in New Jersey. After the photo shoot, the kitten visited our offices in New York, where she was adopted by Chamberlain Bros. editor Anna Cowles and her fiancé, Fritz.

The kitten was named Bridget in honor of the Brooklyn Bridge, and she now happily resides in a lovely apartment in downtown Manhattan, where she spends her days playing with ribbons and tinsel balls, napping with her owners, and looking out the window at the Brooklyn Bridge. She can't wait for her first Christmas.